SACRED ERRAND

in Aboriginal Australia

JOHN J. HARKEY

For John and Twyler

Best wishes from the author

Jon

Publisher's Information

EBookBakery Books

Author contact: sacrederrand@gmail.com

Cover art and design by John J. Harkey

Afterword by Brett Galt-Smith

Author photo by Christine Cerny-Hoffmann

ISBN 978-1-938517-58-7

1. Fiction. 2. Memoir. 3. Travel. 4. Aboriginal Religion. 4. History.

While elements in this memoir have been fictionalized, some characters are based on real people, and are correctly named. Their quotes are used with the speakers' permission.

Warning: culturally sensitive material.
Women and uninitiated men may not wish to read further.

Acknowledgments

My thanks go to the many people who personally shared or informed my journey. In Australia: Robert Bednarik, Helene Albrecht Burns, Graeme Calma, Colin Campbell, Christine Cerny-Hoffmann, Marita Ah Chee, Philip Clarke, Gary Cole, E. Broese van Groenou, Henk Guth, Bill Harney, Ken Hanson, Shane Hersey, Jeff Hulcombe, Peter Latz, Valerie Petering, David Raftery, Joseph Runtji, Allen Stanley, Rupert Maxwell Stuart, Long Jack Phillipus Tjakamarra, Jenny Tonkin, and Gus Williams. And in the United States: Shirley Achor, Christopher Anderson, David Clarke, Francoise Dussart, Barnaby Evans, David Freidel, Theirry Gentis, Richard Gould, O. W. "Bud" Hampton, Jeremy Harkey, Susan Haskell, Norman Hurst, Fred Meyers, Yann-Pierre Montelle, Maury Scobee, Jim Zintgraff and Linda Zisquit.

Thank you to those in Australia who, besides sharing my journey, have read and commented on parts or all of my manuscript: Richard Kimber, Philip Jones, John Morton, Simon Pockley, Brett Galt-Smith, Gary Stoll, and Carl Strehlow.

Thank you to those in the United States who have served as readers of the developing manuscript: Jon Berenson, Lee Clasper-Torch, Michael Grossman, Anita Harkey, Shelley Roth, Jim Sanford, Rob Schmidt, John Siceloff, Pam Steager, Ellen Walsh, Steve Zuehlke, the members of Providence's Historical Fiction Writers' Collaborative, MERG, the Men's Eclectic Reading Group, and my family.

My sincere appreciation for the devotion of the staff at museums and public libraries in Adelaide, Alice Springs, Canberra, Darwin, New York, and Providence, and to the Rhode Island Council for the Humanities, the Central Land Council, Central Australian Stolen Generations and Families Aboriginal Corporation, and the Strehlow Research Centre.

The story I tell here would never have become a book without the talent and perseverance of my writing coaches and editors: Thomas D'Evelyn, Victor Wildman, and Lauren Sarat. You each have my deep appreciation and gratitude.

Mark Hafford, the narrator of this memoir, and the story he tells, while fictionalized, are rooted in the author's own experiences in Australia. My thanks go to the characters in this story who appear under their own names and to the others who have had their names changed. Some characters are entirely fictional. Historical events and their actors are presented as accurately as possible.

DEDICATION

To my parents,
William Jarrott Harkey and Anna Marie Siceloff Harkey.

SACRED ERRAND

The mask of an old man is as indecipherable at first glance
as a sacred stone covered with occult symbols:
it is the history of various amorphous features
that only take shape, slowly and vaguely,
after the profoundest contemplation.
Eventually these features are seen as a face,
and later as a mask, a meaning, a history.

Octavio Paz, Labyrinth of Solitude

I, Elizabeth The Second
By the Grace of God Queen of Australia
Do grant and assign the following Armorial Ensigns:
A Wedge tailed Eagle wings elevated
Grasping with its talons
An Australian Aboriginal stone Tjurunga proper.

Coat of Arms, Northern Territory

1

USTRALIA. I was going to Australia. To the city of Adelaide, and most importantly, to the museum there. Folded in my pocket, on a scrap of paper, was the museum director's name. What I had been told, all that I knew of the man, was that he had access to the Aboriginals. The moment I handed him my father's stone, the *tjurunga* lying at my feet, my task would be done.

When the beverage cart arrived at my row, I received a fresh plastic stem and a pair of minis, two more Barossa Valley Merlots. I watched out my window and sipped my wine. The sun seemed to be stalled below the horizon, was taking forever to begin the new day. I was also slow in taking up my father's errand, and who could say if I was not too late. "Don't delay," a scholar had urged me: The Aboriginal men who understand and might receive the tjurunga stone are few and elderly.

Bruce Chatwin's *The Songlines* lay open alongside my Moleskine notebook. Onto the notebook's first page I had copied out Chatwin's remark, his estimate of a tjurunga stone's importance, *the aboriginal's holy of holies.* And above his words were my father's, found among his papers, for the tjurunga he had taken away thirty years before, *someday it should go home.* My notebook's remaining pages were blank.

I was forty years old, had been married – no kids resulting – and after we split up I'd been stacking on the weight. The trousers I wore still fastened at the waist, but just. My seatmate, an older woman, set out three chocolate bon bons from her gift box. Embracing one with her lips, she slid it in, all the while studying my Moleskine, the way

1

my pen hovered over its empty pages. And rolling the morsel over her tongue, she assembled a smile and said, "You're a writer, aren't you?"

"No. I teach photography. I'm a photographer and the problem with this," I held up my notebook, "no auto-focus." I barked a laugh. She turned over a page in her magazine.

But I told the lady about my mission to Australia, about the tjurunga stone and the frightful taboos attached to it. Our plane was not yet in Australian airspace so no jinx in bringing it out for a look – a crude presence in this upholstered fuselage, and heavy. It strained my tray table. She cocked her head for a glance.

"My father... well, he died," I told her. "It's been a long time. 'This is for you,' he said. He gave me this."

She made another little smile. Then, moistening her fingertip, she turned toward her magazine.

"What he told me right before he died," I started again — and this is how I'd begun to remember it, " 'Son,' he said, 'here is my stone. Take it home cause I never got around to it and now you know I can't.' You see, I'm here because of Dad. And, of course, the Aboriginal man, or people, or whoever, who lost this stone." I raised a little toast to Dad. Now perked up, her lips bloomed as a smile.

She crooned, "Such a gesture. Did you hear, Peter? Isn't that the nicest thing? And all the way from America. Imagine!" And turning to me, she offered her hand. "I'm Penelope. But everybody calls me Penny."

Her husband Peter was a tall man, very tall. His legs already jostled by the cart, he had folded them in. In reply to his wife, he pressed his bushy eyebrows together.

She confided to me, "I lost something once."

"Born into loss," I waved my goblet, "and to suffer from it." Sloshy jocularity, but is it not true? We are constantly hurting from some loss, a dear friend, a diamond, a day. No matter what else we gain, we are left unhealed.

What Penny had lost, she told me, was Peter's family crest. He had it imported for her, a centuries-old plaque carved from a single block of stone. Peter came from a family of Dutch traders who had been shipping to and from Indonesia back when Australia's fronting shore was called New Holland. Peter had captained a ship in the Royal Dutch line when he and Penny met and married. This happened before the Second World War. She left her home in Perth and they built a fine house in Singapore, on a hill overlooking the harbor. Not thinking how fast the world could change, Penny had the stone plaque cemented into the wall at the front of their house.

Then came the "Jap" bombing of Singapore, and the carnage. Penny and Peter watched from their veranda as the city blazed. She told me about their escape on Peter's ship, slipping out at night between hulks burning in the harbor. All this Penny related simply as matters of fact. Her emotions surfaced only when she spoke about the stone left embedded in the wall, about how much it had meant to Peter.

"I've gone back," she sighed, "to request only that, but high gates have been installed, large dogs are on duty, and there isn't a bell or a name. So you see, we appreciate what you are doing, Peter and I. Because it's what we want, too. Isn't that so, dear?"

And then Peter muttered, without opening his eyes, "I take exception, my love, a considerable exception to any comparison between the affection of my family for its noble crest and the Aborigines' attachment to their sordid little relics." I put my stone back onto the floor.

"But, dearest, everyone has mementos they won't let go of."

Flicking his fingers in my direction, Peter said. "I saw it myself, how primitive it is, the stone and the scrawls. The way these people came to idolize that thing, a rock. Terrible taste. I'm just appalled."

Peter gathered up his limbs and turning to face me added, "Before the church arrived, the native moral condition was abominable, wholly undeveloped." Husbands, he claimed, put little value upon the chastity of their wives. And a father "might kill his child just to satisfy his hunger." He was rapping out his words on Penny's tray table. "The Australian Aborigine represents the cursed root of humanity's vine."

The cabin suddenly seemed to have turned humid and close. I reached overhead and twisted open my air nozzle.

Peter conceded that the Aboriginal people represented a stage of savagery from which a higher man might yet evolve. But he had doubts.

"Not even evolution has sufficient patience to advance these people." And he smirked.

Peter resettled his feet into the aisle and cast his eyes back at me, "Do you think you will be doing them a favor by returning a token of their degenerate past? Better to leave them alone."

"It was really my father's idea," I offered and immediately felt that I had betrayed someone – my father or the Aboriginals or myself. I could say nothing in defense of the Aboriginal people, whom I had seen only in pictures, none of which seemed to contradict what Peter was saying. From my father's library I had taken a book about early humans, *Man the Tool-Maker*. It cited the Australian Aborigine as an aspect of mankind's heritage, as exemplars of our universal "Stone Age." The book's only photographic illustration was of an Aboriginal man. Shaggy headed and black-skinned, he squatted in shorts in the middle of nowhere, striking two rocks together between his legs.

It was not my affair, neither who the stone's original owner might have been or what would happen after the museum received it. I found my voice and addressed Peter, "They might be satisfied with who they are." And then speaking for my father, "They ought to have what is theirs. Regardless." Peter set his jaw.

Penny whispered, "My husband is a little old fashioned, but I still think what you're doing is a jolly nice thing. Our natives have lost so much. Poor souls. They're dying out, you know. Not the types in Sydney. The wild ones. We've tried more than once to save and promote the useful kind. I suppose there is only so much one can do."

2

DALLAS, TEN YEARS BEFORE.

I had flown home to tend my father in his final days. The house was silent, as though he were away on one of his over-sea journeys, long spells for a boy waiting for his return. His bathrobe was no longer set out for a morning ramble, and his slippers had been packed away. He slept through most of the days and nights.

During his wakeful moments I sought out any emotion I felt we might share. I made promises of reunion with his wife and daughter whom he would find waiting on the other side, although neither of us believed. I brought out an old photograph of his parents, the hand-tinted rouge still vivid on their cheeks. His gaze fixed past them out the window. From memory, I retold one of his stories, the one from the Outback; his light plane forced down by weather. "This naked family came walking toward you out of the desert. The old man carried a boo-merang, and a spear over his shoulder, a lizard skewered on its tip. You flew him into the air, remember, Dad? He gave you this boomerang." And, as he might have for friends, I held the weapon up to show off its dark, fine-grained wood, its long graceful curve. But the story was his, not mine. He was the one with stories to tell.

There was nothing I could do, little I could offer.

Among those who stopped by were several members of the Petro-leum Society. They told me that he had been "one of their best," a "fire in the hole" oil prospector from the old school when "computer" was the title for a man who interpreted his own raw data. Here was a man, they assured me, that any son must surely admire.

On one of these afternoons, I returned home refreshed and ready to resume the "watch" when a stranger, a man about my age, stepped out of our house. His blue jeans were pressed so that the creases buckled stiffly at his boots, a new Stetson fit squarely over his fresh haircut. He had, as I later learned, worked with Dad in the West Texas oil business. He looked at me. "I didn't know that Mr. Hafford had a son," and he held my arm for a moment, very firmly, "but I want you to know that your dad has been like a father to me."

Coming inside, I stood behind his pillow and studied his sheeted body, his hands – *our* hands, I thought – rising gently up then down on his belly.

He whispered, "Mark."

"Yeah, Dad."

"Mark?"

I stepped forward. "Here, Dad."

"My sash. Bring it to me."

The drab twill band, his bandolier of Boy Scout merit badges, was kept rolled with tissue in his sock drawer. I slid it under his cold fingers, the dozens of embroidered medallions on parade: a war-bonneted Indian head, a winged totem pole, a book opened wide under a flaming gold torch; each representing an achievement toward attaining the Scout ideal. His ways of getting along, it seemed to me, radiated out like concentric rings from this node of integrity.

"Now," he said, "the tjurunga stone." The word came from deep inside his chest, sounding "cher-UNGA." He kept it on a shelf in his office with other souvenirs from around the world. A flat oval stone large as a paddle blade, it dominated his collection not with its ornamental qualities but by its mass, a fragment of some ruin. For a few moments he held the tjurunga stone against his stomach, feeling its burden, a dear one, then he fixed his eyes on me. And as though giving me a part of himself, he said, "This is for you." I reached down for the gift and lifted it away. I set the stone aside.

Then, silence, a foretelling of his next journey. Finally, my father said, "I want to go home."

I knew that "home" meant Poblado, the Central Texas village where he was conceived and born and raised, the place that meant more to him than any other.

Through it flows a creek, Poblado Creek. It's really just a piddly prairie drainage sustained by a spring, but it runs through my grandfather Marcus's patch of earth, his holy estate, and that creek, in his life, was for him the Living Water.

A photograph hangs in the Poblado museum. It shows a couple dozen people assembled alongside the creek: folks from town and country, both black and white, my father as a barefoot boy in suspender shorts, women wearing ankle-length dresses and straw hats, and a pair of harnessed mules. Up to his knees in the deepest part of the creek is Reverend Marcus Hafford. He is standing with a man and a boy suited in white shirts and workaday coveralls. Marcus is bending over, reaching down for an anointment of the creek's Living Water.

Marcus believed that a man could not be a wholesome farmer unless he were a religious man, a fellow craftsman of God, exalted. I can easily see him, my grandfather, mid-week in the fields, knees in the dirt with his farmers, reciting the twenty-sixth Psalm, "Thou visitest the earth, and waterest it: thou greatly enrichest it with the river of God, which is full of water."

"You know we need the rain but, please God, not too much." This society, in which the families toiled on an animate earth alongside an active God, as though fulfilling a myth, would prove to be a delicate fabrication.

Poblado Creek's perpetual spring had for millennia attracted life. Indians lived off immense herds of deer, flocks of turkey, bison, antelope and even bear. It's said that wild honey filled every hollow tree. Nowadays the creekside is divided into exclusive compounds. "Posted" signs are nailed to trees along the water's course: "This Creek Is Private Property. Keep Out." The farmers' fields still yield corn, but the farmers' abandoned homes, now circled close around by enormous combines, are haunted by crows. In Central Texas you might assume that the spirit had gone out of the land, that the land was no longer alive.

Even so, I had seen my father become a different person when revisiting its sites, remembering his father and mother and, no doubt, pleased that the trajectory of his life had never diminished his love for this quiet place. There was a confirmation that seemed to come to him from the earth itself, from the cactus and the oak, the limestone ledges and the water that runs over them. Years after his own father's death, Dad would sit on this bank. I had seen him talking to the creek, and listening. This is where we held his service.

Halfway across the stream, I turned to my family, all of them resolute Texans. My father was the eldest child of seven, the most beloved; throughout his life they called him "Brother." I said a few words about their growing up here, and their modest house long since gone. I said what everyone already knew, and nothing more. Aunt Mimi slipped her shoes off, and she came alongside me. Others stepped into the stream and soon the urn was empty.

My father's first discoveries were made in Poblado, when he was a boy. Spring evenings, stepping across freshly turned furrows, he would watch for the low sun to glint off a flaked arrowhead. He had awoken then, at an edge of history, finding that his mother and father were only the most recent ones to settle there. While the man did not become the treasure-hunting archaeologist the boy had imagined, he remained an enthusiast all his life. He proved again and again that profound human history often lay covered only by a thin layer of dirt. My father gathered up objects into his life, his only excavating tools a watchful eye and the edge of his boot.

My father had been a geophysicist, and a chief at that. He ran crews in the world's remote corners, exploring the earth's deep, hidden contours. Fixed to his office wall was Dad's world, a map spotted with age. On it was a web made with taut red threads that stretched from one country to the next marking his flights that, after touchdown, looped figure-eights into the blank interiors, then returned again to the glue spot of Dallas. On the day after his service, I packed up the sundry artifacts that filled his shelves, to take back with me to New England.

I folded the map and lay it on top of all the rest, then sponged a strip of paper tape to seal the box. A decade would pass before I was ready to open it again.

I carried the box of Dad's artifacts up my basement stairs and set it onto the floor. The brittle tape snapped apart with a tug, and out of the open box came an odor like bone dust. The potency of Dad's stories, I thought they were gone, I thought they had died with him, but as I began to finger through his things, the presence of his exploits came alive. They seemed to occupy the air around me. I lifted out a hide and sinew purse of charms, a wildebeest horn, an Egyptian glass bottle and a handful of oyster-shell currency. I lay them down. Here were the Stone Age axes, massive and deeply faceted, left behind in a Saharan cave when the advance of desert drove the game and their hunters away. There was a petrified pomegranate, thin-walled and plump with stone seeds, the Roman coin he found wedged into a chink on an Asian caravan route, the pottery vessel pulled from a mound in Belize, and wedged below all that was the tjurunga stone.

And there was his "Memoir." I pulled at the packet's string and released a raft of unbound pages along with several sheets of 35mm slides, one filled with shots taken in Australia, and a tape recording.

The cassette was labeled "Freidel." I remembered the name, Dr. David Freidel. He was a prominent professor of archaeology whose off-campus work required him now and then to open a royal tomb in the Mayan jungle. He is the type that my dad as a boy idolized, what he had wanted to be. I fetched my player and slid the tape inside.

Freidel was discussing a box of clay fragments my father had recently brought home from his work site in Belize. I knew the story: Trees are toppled to make way for a convoy of trucks, the damp jungle floor rudely exposed to hard light. Roots that had penetrated the joints of an ancient stone wall are yanked out and a shallow cavity is revealed. My father jumps down to reach in with one hand, and then with two, pulling out a humble prize – a pottery vessel now reduced to shards.

9

Uncannily, Dad's voice entered the room: "I had about five minutes to grab what I could before they went off and left me." And the voice of Dr. Freidel trailed behind, "Well, it looks like you grabbed the right parts."

The broken edges were meticulously rejoined until, finally, resting in Dad's hands was a cylindrical vessel, something that once held incense as it burned, and affixed to it was a deity mask, a wrinkled snaggle-toothed face. It had been buried by the Maya to facilitate the gods' cycle of rebirth, Freidel explained, to maintain their cosmos. Their discussion held no concern for the living Maya who might care for such a deity, who might rebury it to further its obscure purpose, so the deity was retired to my father's office. It was put up on a shelf.

As the tape continued running on, the conversation shifted to Australia. My father had another artifact, one more that he wanted to discuss. And when I realized it was the tjurunga, I stopped the tape and lifted the stone onto my lap. The large and heavy oval was no longer just the fragment of rock that I remembered. Now there was something more. I saw patterns cut into the stone, precisely arranged. In the center was a large spiral, its bands winding inward round and round like a clock spring, terminating at a central node. And four sets of concentric circles were positioned at the stone's cardinal points, all knitted together by arcing lines. The workmanship was precise. The markings were perfect, perfect in graphic simplicity, and perfectly cryptic in whatever message was intended.

I pressed PLAY again, and the reel lurched forward. I bent toward the mechanism. Dad was telling Dr. Freidel how the stone had been acquired, near another work site "in the land around Alice Springs where there was located...." but the tape spooled out mid-line. I jammed REWIND and played it again, with the same result.

Shuffling through the pages of Dad's Memoir, stopping near its middle, I read, "In 1960 I settled for a spell in Australia." Here he recounts how he brought his family to Adelaide, a southern coastal city, as a base to do his work in the interior. I was ten years old, and all this was still quite vivid. Condensing my most memorable year into one sentence, Dad writes, "Mark was enrolled at Prince Alfred Preparatory."

And there was a slide of me taken on my eleventh birthday wearing school-issue gray wool double-breasted jacket and shorts, along with the cap, maroon striped tie and a goofy grin.

Then I found what I was looking for, Dad's account of how he came upon the stone, in "the land around Alice Springs where there was located the remote Lutheran mission of Hermannsburg." The tjurunga stone, he was told at the mission, had been abandoned there after being "pilfered from Ayers Rock by an early explorer." Ayers Rock, he notes, is a renowned site of great power for Aboriginal people. He had selected the stone, which was "better preserved than others," from a camel's saddlebag. A brass buckle, a tongue of parched leather that broke off when he tugged it, proved that Dad was the first person in decades to lay eyes on the antique contents. But nowhere in the memoir does he say who the bag had formerly belonged to, how it got into the hands of the Lutherans, or who at the mission had told him the story of the theft.

Instead, he writes that Aboriginal men had venerated the tjurunga stone "like the finger bone of a saint" – a phrase, I have no doubt, gleaned from Dr. Freidel.

He writes that, "The stone should go home." There was nothing more.

That was unlike my father, to leave a good story unfinished, to end a tale without a satisfying conclusion. And what did he mean by "home?" What home, whose home? Further, had my receiving the "gift" of his stone ten years before obliged me in some way? He hadn't meant for me to set out for Australia, had he? Was this his inner Boy Scout rising up when he was so near his end? It was all too improbable, much too messy, nothing I could think about, not now. I returned the tjurunga to its box and once again set the stone aside.

3

D R. FREIDEL ANSWERED my email right away. He distinctly remembered my father and having been excited about the Mayan deity vase. Did he recall his exchange with Dad about the tjurunga stone? Indeed, he did. Might he be able to help me get the stone back to Australia? "Yes. And I know who to consult."

He named his university colleague Lewis Binford. Freidel wrote, "Lew is a world famous expert in hunters and gatherers" and that *Scientific American* had named him as "quite possibly the most influential archaeologist of his generation." I sent Freidel a photograph of the stone and one week later he wrote back to say that Binford had eagerly taken up the case of Dad's tjurunga, pursuing his contacts in Australia. Why, I wondered, would these two preeminent professionals take such an interest in this curio?

"Lew is convinced," Freidel continued, "that you have a very special tjurunga. He has one particular Aboriginal friend who is an Elder and very wise about the sacred materials of his people, perhaps one of the last two men with the sacred knowledge of these objects." Lew believed, Freidel wrote, that the stone's engraved designs would indicate its human source.

I waited a week for Freidel's next email. When it came, I read that Dr. Binford, attempting to re-engage his Aboriginal friend through an anthropologist in Australia, learned that the elderly man had "met his end." The death of Binford's friend became a greater concern to him than the disposition of my father's stone, and that was the last I heard about the venerable Lewis Binford until *The New York Times* obituary that reported on his death. As quickly as my hopes for an easy resolution had been raised, they collapsed.

How preposterous that Dr. Binford thought he might throw a ringer on his very first attempt, that the stone's owner might be located, even that there was an owner at all.

Freidel remained sympathetic to my father's wish, but now he set my endeavor in a new context. It is from him that I learned the word "repatriation." Those were the first decades after UNESCO called for the return of cultural property, the headiest years of a global effort to recognize the rights of owners to their displaced materials. Another word, "fraught," soon entered my vocabulary.

Anticipating the difficulties that I now faced, Dr. Freidel wrote, "I hope you're not in too much of a hurry with this," then added, "Don't delay. The men today who can read this stone and name its origins are old. They will soon be gone."

Appended to this, Freidel's final email, were the names of a couple of his colleagues in Australia and a wish. "Good luck."

Friedel's two contacts quickly expanded into a multitude of names, authorities in universities and museums whom I peppered with questions. The replies from Australia were immediate, and they were riveting.

The first brought an upbraiding, as the phrase *tjurunga stone* was not used by the academic set; instead, they routinely employed two other words: *secret* and *sacred*, as in "*secret sacred* object." This is what a tjurunga is called by non-Aboriginals if, that is, it must be referred to at all. Theatrical, is what I thought. This is theater.

A female anthropologist received one of my inquiries – an envelope that, as I had noted on the flap, contained a photograph of the stone. It was returned to me unopened and accompanied by a scolding. I had nearly exposed her to that which she, being a woman, must never see. Point taken. Specifically asking for a photo was a male anthropologist: "I am bound with Aboriginal groups of the Western Desert to privacy and respect of secret-sacred laws, so there is no legal problem with that." These darkly charismatic anthropologists straddling at once the primitive and academic worlds posed as arbiters for the uninitiated.

At home I was free to show the stone around as I pleased, including to women who I knew would be amused by the bias against them. This went down in different ways, but I could glimpse each time the power of a secret entwined with the sacred. Yes, there was the tingling that came from toying with taboo, but the stone also woke something darker in my friends, something dormant: remorse for transgression perhaps, wounds from punishment, fear of the primitive and, inevitably, there was the shame-felt trial of temptation.

My letters abroad routinely requested anything that would give me a handle on the stones' backstory. I learned that researchers who had written intimately of secret-sacred matters had had to withdraw their books, or seen them banned. The head of the Anthropology Department at South Australia's Museum of Cultures answered my request, "The literature you ask for is hard to come by."

Some replies included a forbidding, if unspoken, message: "Don't get involved." Nosing around in the natives' religious realm, one letter warned, held the danger of committing an "offense." Was *offense* a matter of etiquette or calamity? There was something odd in the caution. It made my skin crawl.

"Go to the American Museum of Natural History," I was advised, Teddy Roosevelt's pride in New York City. There I would find a collection of Aboriginal sacred objects on view. From the subway stop on Central Park West, I bounded up the museum's inner staircase to the Gallery of Oceanic Cultures. The glass case "Australia," twelve feet long and four feet wide, housed only a tiny diorama in one corner: miniature clay figures acting out hunting, gathering, and fire-making, but nothing about the religious life could I discern.

"Where are the tjurunga?" I later wrote to the curatorial staff. "Removed to Storage," came the reply. "Hottest things we've got. Tjurunga are the only objects in our collection that we cannot display." The museum, apparently, had received a memo from half the world away and heeled to its demand. For his museum's cringing stance, the old Rough Rider may be scowling from the grave. But I was intrigued by the attention that tjurunga commanded, and more than a little unnerved by my stone's mounting gravitas.

As I sat home sealing envelopes and waiting for replies, I began to consider a trip to Australia. I dreamt up a pretty vision, a little scene not yet fully imagined but in outline. I would be presented to a representative of the Aboriginal people whose stone I had recently carried off an airplane. I would hand it over and for a while we would talk about things of importance, for instance, my father's wish that the stone go home, and in turn, the man would share some of his thoughts about this treasure newly restored to his people. I could go when my college was on holiday break.

So I began to cast about for sponsorship. I learned that there were funds for repatriations, but at this time only for Aboriginal skeletons long ago taken to European museums. I wrote to my cousin Maury, the right-hand man to Billy Graham in North Carolina, asking if the evangelist might like to sponsor the return home of "this rather unprepossessing stone, one of man's holiest of objects." Maury wrote back, "It's amazing how this ancient tribal rock has 'fallen' into y'alls hands!! I really am behind you 100%, Mark. Unfortunately," he added, "Mr. G. is currently raising 35 mill $ for a summer revival in Amsterdam," and he could not be diverted to another project. "Now, we can't outgive God when it comes to helping other folks," Maury continued, "but I can personally send you $100 in two weeks." I told him to hold onto his check, and that his kindness would not be forgotten.

Somehow I would manage this on my own; I would personally see the stone home to Australia. I wanted to honor my father in this modest way. But whether the tjurunga was placed into the hands of some particular Aboriginal person or into a museum as part of Australia's officially articulated patrimony was an issue that he left completely open. So it was up to me to decide.

From Parliament House in Canberra, The Honourable Peter McGauran, Minister of Aboriginal Affairs, typed out a letter to me: "Ritual objects are of high significance to all Australians, but particularly so to our indigenous peoples." He continued, "Your proposal to return the tjurunga to its tribal owners shows character and should be a model for others to follow."

McGauran's letter bucked me up. But how was I to reconcile his words with the prospect envisioned by my final correspondent, his letter arriving too late for second thoughts? It said, "Once in Aboriginal hands, there is a fair chance that the tjurunga will be sold to American dealers within weeks of its return." Then he added, "Ultimately, the final decision rests with you as you are now the entrusted keeper of this sacred item. It may be better off remaining in your hands."

To receive the stone I had already chosen the Australian Museum in Sydney, where my plane would first touch down. Sweetening my journey's prospect was nostalgia; I would go next to Adelaide, to see my chum Allen, and revisit my family's home from thirty years before.

Before launching off for Australia, I needed to make a visit back to Texas. Because of my dad's affection for his old friend, I called ahead to Hubie Zintgraff. I told him what my father had left me with, what I was about to undertake. He said, "Come on over."

The Dallas Museum of Natural History sits aside an artificial pond, crowded by fan frond palm trees and enormous live oaks. The Hall of Native Cultures is Zintgraff's domain. Here display cases hold his trophies, simple artifacts salvaged from the ancient Pecos River Indian caves, objects that had been overlooked by pot-holers when digging for artifacts was a pastime, days when the dust raised by amateurs' shovels poured out of those caves like smoke from a massive fire. At the end of the hall, around a corner, was the Collections Department and its door was open. The old white-hair rose straight from his chair and stepped forward to greet me.

"Mark," he said, "I miss your dad. We were alike in some ways, he and I, maybe ways that you two weren't. I respect the difference."

Then a smile crossed his face. "You know your daddy's the one taught me how to pick arrowheads off a field of random stone. It was a lesson from his growing up in Poblado." The old man bent himself over at the waist with his arm leveled off to the horizon. "The sun's got to be real low down to catch a flash off the flint. You've got to keep your eye right on it so it won't disappear." He duck-walked a couple of steps and his hand snatched up an imaginary object. He eyed it for a second, then gingerly placed it back where he had found it.

Zintgraff gave me essential advice. He said, "Don't stop in Sydney. Go on to Adelaide where you're headed anyway. I can give you the name of a man, the director of the Museum of Cultures. He's different from most. Radical, in fact. Opened up a channel between the country's white perimeter and the Aboriginal Center. He's the one who'll get your stone through."

Mr. Zintgraff walked me down to the museum gift shop where he wrote out the man's name on a strip of cash register tape: Christopher Anderson. He bought me a little gift too, a palm-sized Moleskine, and he said to me, "Take notes." I promised him that I would.

4

ALLEN PETERSON stood waiting for me at Adelaide Arrivals. The skinny kid up a tree, waving me goodbye some thirty years ago, now sported a pillowy mustache and, like myself, he had thickened at the waist.

"Your mom, how is she," I asked.

"At the moment, a bit miffed. An Aboriginal spokesman is threatening to gum up the Olympics unless the Prime Minister issues *the apology*. Stolen Generation stuff."

"And your little girl?"

"Three of them now, and not so little. Whip smart, entirely to their mother's credit. All redheads. You'll see them later."

He took my satchel. "Heavens, man, what have you got in here – *rocks?*" The jibe came with a familiar impish smile. He knew it was a rock. Everything had been explained when I called him from the States. Allen was now an anthropologist at Adelaide University. He liked this idea of returning rather than appropriating what was never really ours, what was theirs. "Long overdue," is what he said. I told him about my flight and Penny's husband Peter, the things he had said. Allen assured me, "I think you will find that many people are supportive," and that the Aboriginal population was in fact not "dying out."

"Stone Agers, though. Right?"

"The Paleolithic was a couple of million years ago. So, no, not technically. The Dreamtime, on the other hand, is ongoing. It's eternal. So I've heard."

"Meaning?"

"Your tjurunga has a home. Potentially. It belongs to a living spiritual system, the Dreamtime."

"And where is that practiced, exactly?"

"Once, the Dreamtime may have spanned the country. But *this* has always had an exceedingly limited range. It's a tjurunga. It came from the Centre."

"Look," he said, stopping at a banner that announced, "Welcome to Oz." It had a cartoon picture of the island-continent Oz-traya. "This map is a meter wide, wouldn't you say? Now place your fist on the very center." I did so. "You just covered the traditional range for tjurunga. Only a day's drive in any direction out of Alice Springs. But it's a big grid."

"Dad's tjurunga is going to the museum tomorrow."

"Yes," said Allen. "That's the ticket."

This day we devoted to revisiting my once upon a time home. I intended to enjoy myself. Half-remembered scenes leaped out: energetic people bustling about, colonial buildings girding the bends of River Torrens, picket-fenced parkways graced with tender gardens of hollyhock and rose. Everywhere I looked I saw the past. I asked Allen if we might stop at Prince Alfred Prep. Standing at the gate, my hands on its iron bars, I peered inside. In the warm, mid-winter light everything about the school appeared vivid and sweet: the blond limestone blocks crafted into arches and balconies, the simple white roses growing over rough fieldstone walls, the Edwardian turrets and chimney towers. A rush of boys in blazers, crimson with gray piping, raced past us for the sports paddock. I stood there, searching their faces. One youngster, a wisp of a fellow with a tangle of blond hair, broke step, slowing down to look back at me, then turned again to rejoin the pack.

On a hill overlooking downtown, Allen parked at a tulip-fringed plaza where an Aboriginal couple sat under the bronze statue of Colonel William Light. Just as I remembered, Light's open palm reached over all he had once surveyed, an Eden, a forested coastal plain and home of the Red Kangaroo people. Now his hand gave benediction to King William Street.

Down on that street I, a new kid in town, had first seen an Aboriginal person. It was 1960 and my father had taken me out of school for a parade, to see young Queen Elizabeth on her first visit to Adelaide.

I was standing beside my dad, who always had his Leica, when he turned toward a group of children and snapped their picture. I still have the Kodachrome slide. In it the children are dressed as though for Sunday School — pleated coats buttoned over blue jumpers and topped off with wool caps. Their shepherdess, a white matron, keeps them in order beside a lamppost festooned with flags. Like everyone else, they are waiting for the royal limousine to appear. Even without Dad's photo, I would have remembered this: the children were black in a white city, and the mold of their faces was unfamiliar and disquieting. It hadn't occurred to me until the release of the film *Rabbit Proof Fence*, who those children might have been. The 1960s were the waning years of forced assimilation of mixed-blood children into the white population. For forty years, children of unwed Aboriginal women, many of them fathered by Territory settlers, had been evacuated out of their apparently dying homeland and put into the care of religious orders. It was an act of salvation, a newspaper reported, even a mercy: "Half-Caste Babies Rescued From the Bush." Who and where were they now? Surely not this woman and the agitated man sitting together on the plaza bench, by the tulip bed, sheltered by Colonel Light's hand.

En route to Allen's house, we detoured into our old neighborhood, its streets of modest tile-roofed bungalows. Kensington remained a white child's perpetual Eden. Almonds lay un-gathered on the streets, and under the shade of orange trees boys still littered the footpaths home from school with perfect coils of peel.

Allen parked along the cul-de-sac where our two front yards once met. While he went to chat with the people living in his old house, I looked around for anything that I might recognize.

I could see the old gum tree had been sawn to the ground. It was up there, in our hideaway, that Allen told me about the Aboriginals' gruesome rituals: fingernails ripped off, penises lacerated root to crown, teeth whacked out of the jaw, and how magicians could point a sliver of bone cut from a dead man's tibia to deliver a withering death to his enemy. There was never anything so wonderfully gory in the classroom. In fact, there was nothing at all about indigenous peoples, and nothing about the white men who once had poison-baited them, or why.

The gum tree was also the perch where Allen would ogle the girl next door, a precocious redhead, through her bedroom window. Allen was a year or so older than me, and always more clever. But this time he got caught.

Allen had to endure a tirade from her outraged father who said that it was theft, an offense that would not heal, at least not easily. "I was only looking," Allen said. And to his own parents he explained, "There were things I needed to know." Retreating to my yard, Allen had confided, "It wasn't just me, she knew what I was doing all the time." Her bedroom curtains, once so easily parted, were quickly stitched together.

Allen beckoned me to the car where, for a moment after switching on the motor, we sat looking through the windshield. He turned to me and asked, "Do you remember Anya?" But before I could reply, he wheeled us back onto the road and we continued our course for the Adelaide hills.

He wanted to tell me about the maturation that anthropology, as a science, was forced to go through. I wanted to know what happened to Anya.

"Since Australia's discovery," he began, "the indigenous of Australia have been exemplars of qualities so far removed from Europeans that comparisons were made in terms of opposites. In your profession, Mark, Aboriginals would be the photographic negative." In the first decades of study, ethnologists had endowed them with a series of preposterous qualities, and from those built theoretical frameworks ranging from the wobbly to the absurd. "There's one superlative in particular," Allen said. "All the others would fall under it: Aboriginal Australians represent the 'absolute bedrock in the scale of civilization.' This was not meant as a slur," he hastened to add. There had been a motive for the ranking. "British ethnologists believed that one might work forward from an uncontaminated race, a race abandoned by time on an isolated island…"

"Like Australia."

"Precisely…the 'operations of the human mind in its upward progress from savagery to civilization.' "

"Aboriginals as living fossils."

"Just so. But Australia was not a 'museum of sociological fossils' any more than our Royal Family would be. Just the same, those proto-anthropologists believed themselves to be headed 'back from the period of recorded history into the dim twilight of far-distant epochs.' "

"Jules Verne. *Journey to the Center of the Earth*."

"Of the period," said Allen. "Or, looking outward, we might say that our natives were the farthest visible galaxy, still quivering from the shock of creation. It's humbling, you know, the abundance of fanciful notions and seductive gossamers produced to support a faulty premise."

Allen pulled off the road and parked beside a wine shop. He swung open his door. "Coming in, Mark? What do you fancy?"

"Anything local?"

"*Lots* of that." Inside, he strode the aisle plucking out a half dozen bottles. Of course I paid, and carried the sack into the car.

Once seated, Allen launched us on a roller-coaster ride up the Adelaide Hills. Not a little jet-lagged, I was suffering. Flying along the Pacific equator, the sun had been nearly arrested by our speed. Now it zipped through the sky, and in a hemisphere where it did not belong. The city was well below us when Allen took the final steep curve and leveled out onto Treetop Terrace. Pulling up to his garage he asked me again, "Do you remember that filly next door to us, the redhead?" and he was out of the car before I could react.

Anya met us at the door wiping her hands on her apron and tucking back waves of still-brilliant red hair. She was middle-aged, and she was gorgeous. As we were shaking hands she looked into my eyes and flippantly remarked, "You two haven't changed a bit, have you?" I blinked. I took her to mean that, as a male, I was implicated in Allen's treetop mischief. Or was she seeing something else that I could not?

Their three girls seemed to fill the house: Rachel ironing her school tunic, Rebecca sawing the cello, and the youngest, Caitlin, was swatting at the air with a lacrosse stick. Rachel was the House Leader this week, and she acted the host. "It's feeding time at the zoo, Mr. Hafford. Care to bog in?" "Don't be boffy," scolded Rebecca. "Nark," was Rachel's retort. "Nong," Rebecca threw back. And we settled, more or less, to dinner.

Afterwards, Allen led me onto the back deck to listen to the wild sounds coming from the wooded ravine below. He named the bird at its every song or outburst: kookaburras, parrots, galahs. Koala bears rustled in the eucalyptus branches and, he assured me, those clawing noises I could hear were kangaroos trying to get at Anya's garden.

"These hills are Adelaide's barrier to the Outback. Begins just beyond the last ridgeline." From Allen's thin strip of humid coast, we looked toward where green fields and running rivers halted at gibber plains, salt flats, and dunes of red sand.

Wasteland, is what I said.

"For the researchers, that *wasteland* held the secrets they most wanted." By the nineteenth century, wherever the coast had been settled, the traditional Aboriginal life had withered or had vanished. Not so in Central Australia. Here, it was thought, humankind's first impulse toward religion might be revealed. Cadres of researchers camped at the ceremonial grounds, sifting out and assaying Aboriginal religious motives. Observations were recorded, and tentative theories proposed: " 'This looks like the beginnings of our baptismal rite by immersion.' So on and so forth."

"A tjurunga," I offered, "is like the finger bone of a saint."

"Yes…somewhat." Gesturing toward my satchel, he said, "This slab you're carrying was esteemed from almost the beginning. Grasping its significance in ritual, you see, could illuminate the entire Aboriginal cosmology."

The Holy Grail for Australian anthropology became decoding the natives' devotion to their tjurunga stones. Then, like with the medieval quests, restraint was not even possible. Researchers claimed them, wherever they were found, for science, in the name of science. So began a plague of plundering – tjurunga stolen, traded, sold. "It's possible that in the midst of all this," Allen added, "that your father's tjurunga was ripped from the hands of those who venerated it."

"My father used the word 'pilfered,' not 'ripped.' "

"My profession brought a terrible burden to the indigenous peoples. Our failure was not respecting the sanctity of the secret-sacred life – the legends, the sacred diagrams, the tjurunga stones themselves. These were entrusted to us. Academic overexposure desiccated it – the culture – taming it into words."

Allen confessed his paranoia that somebody someday was going to confront him. "What happened," he would be asked as though he had been its custodian. "What happened to the world's oldest religion, the root of all mankind's spiritual inclinations? It was here when you arrived. Where is it now? What have you done with it?"

Allen had taken on the burden of his profession's early intemperance just as openly as he had admitted to his childhood act of voyeurism. He rather elegantly draped this weight of guilt across his shoulders. At the time I thought his posture melodramatic, but at least it was filled with life.

"There's an hour still," Allen said as we stepped back inside, "before my performance tonight."

"What performance?"

He and a university colleague had worked up an impersonation of the renowned pair of researchers Sir Baldwin Spencer and Frank J. Gillen, and revived their frontier-days magic-lantern lecture on Aboriginal ceremonial custom. For Allen, telling the old story of predation upon the natives' secret/sacred life was a means for him to soothe his professional conscience. It was also intended to unsettle European-descent museologists. Their institutions, Allen would remind them, once were memorials to imperial power, and their collections: trophies from a conquest of people who had "overstayed their time on earth."

Allen said his skit would begin with Gillen, in 1875, en route to assume management of the Alice Springs telegraph station, wide-eyed for Aborigines. "We are going to have a look at some of them tomorrow," Gillen noted in his diary. Baldwin Spencer, the Oxford-trained naturalist, showed up at the telegrapher's door on the day his scientific expedition to the interior disbanded, in Alice Springs. Theirs was a consequential meeting.

A lively correspondence between the two men ensued, an exchange of raw data from Gillen on Aboriginal practices for Spencer's refined theory. Gillen's letters and rough field notes, sent to the "prof" over four and a half years, narrate their passion for penetrating Aboriginal secrets, as though it were the grandest of treasure hunts. A letter from Gillen might typically include, "We are daily getting deeper into the mysteries of Aboriginal life," or "I am inclined to your idea but will make further enquiry." They were the first to recognize tjurunga stones as the key to understanding everything: the mythological ancestral beings, the inalienability of the Aboriginals from their land, and their devotion to the Law that determined rights and governed ritual. Towards the end of their joint research, Gillen would write to Spencer at his university in Melbourne, "This mail's notes, if they do not entirely elucidate the tjurunga problem, goes so near a perfect solution that I doubt whether we shall get deeper."

Of course, it was the natives who paid for the men's passion. Allen kept a stable of jarring quotations from that bygone era. He gave me a last sample: Gillen wrote Spencer, "I have learnt that a number of *tjurunga* are deposited in a cave known to one of my Niggers and I am about to organize a little expedition to annex the whole collection." Tonight if I could stay awake, Allen promised, I would see for myself.

But the thought of staying awake, even for an hour longer, was unbearable to me. My head was swimming. I was desperate for a bed, and Allen understood. If I should wake after he was picked up and be inclined to join them, he said, his car keys would be left for me. I would have liked to see what he was up to, really, but I was tired, and I slept too late.

I woke to a quiet house, the lights burning. I started the teakettle, sat in the living room and picked up a large picture book. Reproduced inside were some of Frank Gillen's plate-camera photos of tribal types, his "greasy brethren." I flipped past a picture of three unadorned maidens; one of a woman in mourning, her figure caked with white powder; another, a congregation of warriors waving a canebrake of spear shafts in the air. One photo showed a pair of men rubbing two sticks into a fire, another a group portrait of ten young bucks neck-chained in a row, posing with their warden.

A sequence of photos bore the caption "A Sacred Errand." That stopped me. Here were men engaged in the ritualized return of tjurunga lent to them some time before by a neighboring clan. As though falling through the page and into the desert scene, I was there, watching through Gillen's camera. Led by their Elder, a dozen bare-chested tribesmen are high-stepping in single file. The leader holds before him a bundle. Another clan, its Elder also up front, comes opposite, and the two men meet head on. Both brigades drop knees onto the earth, their faces rapt. The men press forward encouraging the two Elders. The bundle, enclosing a tjurunga, is extended. From the other side, empty hands are reaching forward. A car door slams. The Sacred Errand flattens into ink on paper. I looked up from the page, and they were gone, as though those men had never even existed.

Allen stood at the driver's window, clasping the hand of his partner in celebration of a good evening's work. "Huzzahs for the grand old Queen," he said.

"God Save the Queen," came the cheerful reply. The teakettle awoke with a *twee,* and that brought Anya from her room into the kitchen.

When we three had settled to our steaming cups, I asked Allen, "So what will happen tomorrow, when the museum gets my father's tjurunga stone?"

"I like to think that it will be properly passed on, re-sacralized and put back into service. But you'll never know how it's being used. One can't go around peering in like we used to do." He winked at Anya.

"Your father's stone has you at the edge of a vortex spun round by two colliding forces, the tainted reputations of revered men within their august institutions, and the collapse of an incredible but fragile culture. That vortex still carries abrasive memories, painful memories, in suspension."

"Maybe it would be wiser to skip the museum altogether," I proposed, "and just give my dad's stone directly back to the Aboriginal people."

"Don't even think about it," Allen thundered, his dramatis personae suddenly reignited. "That is unheard of." Then, in a conciliatory tone, "The professionals will know what to do with it. Be a good lad and just stay clear. Put your rock in the museum's hands and we'll see that you get packed off neatly. No worries."

5

ALLEN REHEARSED his lecture all the way down the hill while I struggled with my muffin, its crumbs dotting my lap. He asked: Consider an Aboriginal's affiliation with a totemic animal. Was this a social system that regulated sexual relations or was totemism a religious system? He asked: Does totemism exist in Australia at all? Or is the word utterly inadequate? Then how else can you describe an Aboriginal's dynamic relation with ancestral beings and the land they seeded with procreative power? I replied with an occasional nod and a "yes."

He pulled up to the curb, wished me luck at the museum and drove away to teach his first class. I was in downtown Adelaide at the edge of the Culture District. Off the curb stepped a phalanx of dark-suited men marching toward their respective offices. Onto the curb, groups of children tumbled from a rank of buses, waiting to be sorted by their color-coded ribbons. Half the kids, the blue ribbons, went left, heading for the Museum of Cultures. The red ribbons were directed toward the Museum of Art with its columned Greek facade. I found myself at this crossroad between art and ethnology with no color-code to set my path.

During the years that my father kept his tjurunga in his office, occasionally hauling it out for visitors, he would say that the thing was "museum quality." But which museum did he have in mind, the one for art, or the one for artifact? In 1960, the year my father brought us to Adelaide, tjurunga, out of cultural propriety, were no longer exhibited at the Museum of Cultures. But a single specimen had just been put on display in the neighboring museum for a blockbuster show, Australian

Aboriginal Art–Sacred and Secular Objects. The flat, gray stone could not have been much to look at. Just the same, there sat this object in its provocative singularity, and probably my father, his spirit as a collector ignited, standing right beside it.

In this moment of my indecision, a child, a little boy not minding the call from his teacher, separated himself from his mates. He stopped at my side and reached for my hand. We stood this way for only a few seconds, but in these seconds I realized that I had never held a child's hand before. "Sorry," his teacher said. He was tugged away.

I fell in with the kids bound for the Museum of Cultures. In my pocket was the slip handed me some days before by Hubie Zintgraff. He had written on it "Christopher Anderson, Director, South Australian Museum of Cultures."

Outside the still-locked entrance, the mob of children gathered at the glass doors, poised for their rush inside. I stood opposite the uniformed attendant who stood indifferently inside by his watch clock. I used the interval to review my morning's task.

According to Zintgraff, Anderson's museum contained the world's largest collection of Aboriginal sacra, and this director had made a name for himself by returning these objects to their former owners. Zintgraff had met Anderson years before at a conference in New Orleans where Anderson lectured on his experience mediating "the vexed problem" of reconciling men, museums, and their sacred objects.

At the Museum of Cultures Anderson de-emphasized the curatorial sanctity of "things" and instead used them to build cross-cultural relationships. He believed that was the "Aboriginal way." His work was patient, meticulous and ultimately rewarding for all concerned. This was the man who could broker the placement of my father's stone.

At precisely ten o'clock, the museum doors parted, and I was swept inside on the surge of kids. I landed hard at the reception desk and held fast. A young attendant, who wore a new brass badge on his jacket breast, could not find Anderson's name in the personnel directory.

"Ain't here," he shouted over the din. "You got the name right?" Then an older guard, a stout, mustachioed gentleman sauntered over, his badge worn down by years of polishing. He said, "Anderson left two years ago." I fell back a step. "E's with Normandy Mining, writing contracts with the Aborigines."

The younger man demanded, "You made an appointment with im?" Who was the more daft, he for asking or me for not having done so? I explained my purpose. "I've come from America to bring home a sacred object, a tjurunga stone. I want to see your director, please." The two men looked at each other.

"Not ere, neither, sir," repeated the older one, his gaze on me now sharpening. "I'll be pleased to take that object from you, sir. And we're most appreciative, I'm sure, that you've come by."

Who else in the administration, I asked, might I speak with?

I had my answer minutes later, time enough for all the children to crowd deep inside and several galleries away. "You're to see the Registrar," said the older attendant who set off with me at his heels. I followed him up the grand staircase, ascending past an immense glass window stained five hues of blue, one for each of the seas that caress Australia's shores. Topping the stairs, we entered a great hall, the gallery of Oceanic Cultures.

This salon was unchanged since the days when museum collections were acquired from voyagers who bartered with natives on island beaches, and the curator's job was to make decorative arrangements of the booty. Tall arched glass cabinets, each labeled for an island of origin – Papua New Guinea, Borneo, Sumatra, Java, New Caledonia, and more – stretched down both sides of the long hall. Inside the cabinets were sportingly displayed regiments of totem figures, fans of royal staffs and war clubs, peacock tails of canoe paddles, sunbursts of spears and rosettes of masks hung artfully around brilliantly decorated shields.

My guide, slowing to recover his breath, rested a shoulder against a rack of human skulls, the Solomon Islands display. He said, "This ere's what the Aboriginal gallery looked like before they tore it out. What you've got in your bag there, you'd have seen many of em. Took em off display in the sixties, ya see, when the Abos began payin visits." He headed for a construction barrier onto which a plywood door had been hinged. "Straight through here, sir. Do mind your head."

Demolition of the old exhibit hall was long finished and construction of the new Australian Cultures Gallery was underway. Carpenters were completing video console cabinets while electricians wired motion-activated audio zones. Visitors were to encounter an electronically simulated Aboriginal presence.

A rear-lit photograph flickered to life as I passed it. It was an enlargement of a snapshot showing five barefoot Aboriginal men. They wore western hats, and their shirts had come un-tucked from reaching overhead as they added paint to a mural, some sort of tribal design.

The light behind the photograph blinked off, and a voice cried out as if bitten, "Aiee! Bugger!"

I hurried to catch my guide at another stairwell and followed him down until we came to its end. Here was the repository for everything removed from the gallery above. It was as quiet as a cave and illuminated only by a string of safety-yellow construction lamps running down the center. "That's your man down there."

"Where?" I asked, turning to find the guard already moving up the stairs.

He called out, "At the back."

I walked from one pool of light, through the intervening darkness, into the light again, passing by odd forms shrouded with dust cloths. No sign of the Registrar, or even of his office. There was only, at the end, an immense canvas tent. I yelled into the virtual twilight, "Who's there?"

"Hello, yourself," came a man's voice, muffled yet resounding in the hall.

"Hello?"

"Yes, yes. I'm here." A canvas door flipped open and a wash of warm light spilled across the floor. His other arm beckoned me in. "Dear me, it's so late," he said although it was still morning. "No time to waste. Come in."

I ducked under the flap and found a well-ordered refuge. The tenant, an elderly gentleman, resumed his seat behind a wooden field desk. The string of construction lights ended exactly here, its last bulb shaded with a paper map of Australia. The center of the country fell close to the filament, which had bleached it a whitish blank.

"You're the Registrar."

"Derrick Pickering," he said, pointing at a chair for me to sit. He was bald, and his brow was furrowed as though for a lifetime he had pulled down hard on a hat, perhaps the derby on the shelf behind him. He dressed in a dark jacket, and his high white collar was cinched up with a tie whose fashion predated my birth. "Come along, sir, what is on your mind?"

I reached into my bag, withdrew the tjurunga, and placed it on the table before him.

"Ah," he said. He picked up the stone, turned it over and back again under the light, and then he pressed it between his palms, concentrating on its form. He rubbed it up and down, gently touching its various surfaces, worn down by other men's handling. There were traces of red ochre rubbed deep into the cuts, even into the stone's grain. "I suppose you'd like us to take this from you," he said.

"Yes, and to get it back to its owners. I was told Mr. Anderson was good at that."

"No doubt you were. Very well. Tell me all you know about the source of this object."

I recited my father's account. It did not take long. Pickering put the stone back on the table and pushed it away. "Thank you, but we're not interested."

Not interested? This was a sacred tjurunga stone, the Aboriginals' holy of holies. How dare he turn up his nose at my father's offering? I was indignant, then angry, ready to lash out at this smug, imperious, colonialist lackey. And enunciating carefully, I began, "Mr. Pickering, isn't it right that..."

"Please, allow me to explain," he added hastily. "You are an American, I believe, and patience may count less for you.

"No one knows how many tjurunga were removed from Central Australia in the last century and a quarter. I have personally registered into our collection around three thousand such objects. Look at these," he said, gesturing to a stack of leather-bound volumes, perhaps twenty in all, and each one was a behemoth. "For every tjurunga brought in from the bush, we made a complete entry – where and from whom it was collected, the man's language group, his skin name, his genealogy, who else was standing around, even the time of day and the weather.

"So, let us say that I had a numbered object in hand that I wanted to send home. I would go to, for example, page twenty of volume six and read 'Cockatoo Creek Expedition, 1930, collected from Old Mick Tjupurulla,' and you could see who his parents were, who his children were, and one could thereby discover who his descendants are."

Okay, maybe Pickering kept better accounts than my father had. A little gumption was all he needed to source mine out. Pickering went on. "For all the information recorded in these volumes, in the thirteen years of Mr. Anderson's tenure, he succeeded in returning to the source's descendants perhaps thirty of these, *thirty* – which you would count a remarkable success if you knew the odds against it. You see, whole family lines have died out."

I had calmed down but was far from mollified. "I was told that the museum would receive this from me."

"And we will, yes. We are known as a keeping place for tjurunga, and I am obliged to accept it. But the company it will keep…"

"What company?"

"Yours will join others that came to us with no provenance. The best we can do is store it with respect. And here it will sleep forever. Is that what you want for your tjurunga?" I made no answer "Very well." He reached forward.

"No," I said. "Look, this is only my second day in the country. I don't know anything about these things. Couldn't you mail it to, I don't know, a tribe somewhere? Let them figure it out?"

"That would be ill-advised, to say the least. Besides, we now find that Aboriginal men come to us."

"They'll come to *you?*"

"In the beginning, it wasn't at all a pleasant experience. Some men were quite adversarial. One of the land councils escorted down a group of Elders and demanded, 'You've got our stuff and we want it back.'

We brought them in but had to tell them, and this was honest, 'Look, we don't know what we've got.' "

"But you said everything was cataloged."

"And that is so, but finding an item is a different thing. A ledger entry might say 'such and such an object,' give its unique number and then something like 'fourth shelf in the sixth cabinet,' a reference to a storage system that hadn't been operating for sixty or seventy years. All across the floor were piles and piles of material dating to 1850 and three thousand Aboriginal sacred objects haphazardly mixed in.

"It would be as though you visited your family crypt and found your parents' whitened bones scattered around the floor. There were tears."

"But you had their stuff, and they wanted it back."

" 'You'll have to wait,' we told them. 'Give us a chance to sort this out.' Chris was hired, and he devoted himself to the task." Pickering hesitated. "Are you finding this at all illuminating?"

"Go on. Please."

"Very well. First Mr. Anderson had to convince the museum board that we were not the owners of these things, but only their custodians. His proposal was based on traditional Aboriginal practice.

"His contention, you see, was that our tjurunga were not given to us forever, but extended as a social act of engagement. Indeed, Mr. Anderson, when he was able to bring these objects back to the Bush, found there was no great surprise that they had been returned. The surprise for everyone here was that he occasionally came back to the museum with more tjurunga than he set out with."

Pickering paused. I repeated his words like a child practicing a magic trick. "He came back with more tjurunga than he set out with. Okay, how'd he do it?"

"He came to be trusted. When Aboriginal men journeyed to Adelaide, they found that their objects were far safer here than what they could maintain in the bush. They would send us their tjurunga for safe-keeping and reclaim them as needed for ceremonial use, returning them again later on."

Holy Jo, I thought: the bare-chested tribesmen's exchange of tjurunga in *A Sacred Errand*. It was Frank Gillen's century-old photograph reenacted with a contemporary twist. I couldn't help myself. I slapped my knee and whooped, "What a development!" And old Pickering was enjoying himself, too. I could see it on his face.

"Well, I never thought I'd...There were moments...," Mr. Pickering gave a little chuckle. "When the cave – that's what the storage vault came to be called, a sacred cave – was first 'blessed' we had all these Elders assembled and the staff burned a torch of herbs to 'smoke' the room. Well, of course, all the alarms went off, and the firefighters came and all the commotion. The old men had a great laugh!"

We both smiled at the image. "Chris could be a bit of a showman. His sense of theater matched theirs. He'd swing a bull-roarer around his head to warn off women who weren't even there. He always approached the cave with this reverential palaver and his big ball of keys that clearly impressed the old men. He'd lock the door behind them and do what he did inside: sit on the floor and bring down whatever objects these men needed to see."

"Where did you say your 'cave' is?"

Pickering pointed toward the canvas flap but recoiled his finger as he recollected how it all had changed. "Dear, dear. Just moments of glory. There was a time when the old men came to us saying, 'These tjurunga are the tools we need to fix things, to get our authority back, to give our young men some sense of who they are, what the *tjukurrpa* is, what it's all about.' "

"Excuse me? The jacuppa what?"

"The *tjukurrpa*. The Dreamtime. The sacred Law." He looked down at his folded hands, sighed and then fell silent.

"Well, okay," I said. "So what do you think I should do with this stone?"

Pickering raised his face and looked up at me with surprise. "Young man, I have worked here for sixty-two years, and this is the first time someone has personally asked me that question."

"You're putting me on, right?"

"Will you join me in a cup of tea?" Pickering stood and flipped a switch on his electric kettle. He wiped the dust out of his extra cup and began to prepare the teapot. "Won't be a moment," he said.

He picked his words carefully. "I know too well the history and consequences of colonialism in the Centre. Theodore Strehlow, in his *Songs of Central Australia*, quotes a native informant on a police massacre in the Centre: 'They came in anger. They shot many people. They took shieldfuls of tjurunga away.'

"I have seen for myself the affectionate regard for tjurunga among men who hold their fathers' memories dear. Have no doubt, sir. These objects are wanted not just for sentimental reasons. The stones are what made – do make – the men real."

And after tea, Pickering rose from his desk. He was stooped and he looked tired. "You know, people assume the safest place in the world for cultural treasures is in a museum." He clutched my arm so that he was leaning on me even as he pressed me forward. "Old Carl Strehlow, the missionary, shipped many tjurunga out of Hermannsburg to the Volkermuseum in Frankfurt Au Main. Dust. They're all dust now. Destroyed in the war. Another tragedy.

"I think I have made my point, have I not? Your tjurunga stone does not belong in our museum. Take it to the desert and fling it into the sand if you must. There have been worse fates for them." He put his hand on my back and gave me a little push. "Get your tjurunga home, young man. Go."

The canvas flap fell behind me cutting off the light from inside. Just as quickly, the warmth of Pickering's convictions flew away. The clutter around me seemed to stretch forever into dimly lighted reaches. Pickering's pathway through this culture, so clear and rational, moral and necessary, all of it was suddenly and totally obscure. It was preposterous the way he suggested that these stones made men real.

Then again, my father's stone had given him a heft I am sure he had always sought; it must have made him far more real, at least to himself. And from his hands into mine. I had no plan now for disposing of his tjurunga, but going in search of its Aboriginal home was not my agenda.

6

THE STATE LIBRARY sits adjacent to the Museum of Cultures. A barrel-vaulted ceiling runs the length of its antique atrium, the mezzanine ringed by a wrought iron balustrade that glitters from gold accents, and alabaster busts of venerated men perch in grottos warmly lit by candelabra.

Down the hushed central aisle solitary visitors were bent over volumes while, behind an oak desk, a staff counselor awaited the opportunity to serve. It felt good here, out of the museum's chaos of competing interests. Everything was calm and in perfect order; there were no worries about where anything belonged. I ambled down the grand aisle with eyes turned upward, my chin leading me forward.

The card catalog sat in the center of the room. I squared off with it and slid out the drawer labeled "th to tra." There was only one card referring to tjurunga. I filled out a request slip and sat down to wait.

Within a few minutes, the attendant handed me back my slip, for the book *Songs of Central Australia* by Theodore Strehlow. The slip was now stamped "Restricted." The director of the library's Aboriginal Collection had penned a note at the bottom: "See me." I set out for the stairwell, still leading with my chin.

Two flights of stairs, the first one of stone, the next wood and a little narrower and darker, led to a door stenciled "Aboriginal Collection." I rapped on the pane of frosted glass.

A figure came forward, stopping short to sweep back her hair. The bolt unlocked, the door opened a crack, I held up the slip.

"Ah, *Songs*." She glanced over her shoulder. "This is Tamara." I leaned into the room, a smile and a nod to Tamara, who was Aboriginal and sitting on the floor. "I'm Andrea," she said and read from the slip, "You're Mr...."

"My name is Mark. Look, if it would be better..."

"Let me explain." Andrea stepped sideways a little, still holding onto the door. "Those songs, in that book," and she gestured to *Songs of Central Australia*, which lay open on Tamara's lap, "These songs were left behind by the ancients who'd first sung the world into existence."

"Oh," I said.

"These songs continue to animate the earth. They're the evidence for the Aboriginal people that they are yet not alone." Andrea looked back at Tamara.

"Strehlow's book is not as restricted as many in our collection are," she said, stepping aside. "But the material *is* sensitive, and I have to be mindful of how others..."

"She means me," Tamara spoke up, "my people. What's in that book is ours."

"That's okay," I said in retreat. "I'm sure there are other..."

"We got that book pulled off the shelves from here to Darwin."

"Really? Well, alright then..."

"You know what moral copyright is? These are *our* sacred songs and just because it's a book don't mean it's open to you. Even all our men can't see that stuff."

"No, I never heard of that. But it's..."

"You write a book using this material without permission, we got lawyers in Sydney."

"Mark's not here to write a book, are you, Mark?"

"Postcards. Only postcards." Hubie Zintgraff at the Dallas Museum, who set me on this odd path, would be the first to hear from me.

"Well then. The important thing here is that Tamara has suffered from the erosion of traditional pathways to cultural knowledge..."

"I was only a little child when they took me away."

"…and through our research…"

"I am a honey ant woman."

"You see, Tamara's mother…"

"Was raped," said Tamara. "By the first white man she ever saw."

Andrea addressed me earnestly, "This woman before you, even in advance of her birth, was a particle of the honey ant ancestor. And that fact is celebrated no matter what the father's totemic affiliation, or lack of one, might have been."

I thought of the man and woman at the plaza, the tulip beds, the bench at Colonel Light's feet. "You're…"

"We're still here."

She closed *Songs* and slid it aside. "Nobody knows the pain our mothers and dads gone through. They died with the pain. They took their pain to their graves. They had no one to speak to. No one listened to them. And their pain is buried with em. You understand that? They was black, nobody wanted to know them." Tamara heaved herself up, stepped past me, and reached for the door. "The white man, they got away with it." The door shut behind her, the glass rattling in its frame. Tamara's footfall on the stairwell faded.

Andrea found me standing in her office. "Oh, Mark. Now, what was it that brought you here? *Songs*?"

I didn't answer her question. Instead, I told her the story of my father's stone, about the "early white explorer" who pilfered it from Ayers Rock, and the unknown person who had lost it. The odds against the tjurunga's return, I now knew, were as poor a prospect as Tamara's, of either finding the way home. But Andrea was immediately engaged, saw it as a puzzle, and presented me with a suggestion. Why not, she proposed, begin with a little detective work. I should look over some of the accounts of early explorers traveling between Ayers Rock and the mission at Hermannsburg, the two sites that figured in my father's story.

Andrea overestimated my ambition. Dad had never gone that deep and I didn't feel obliged to, either. Frankly, Pickering's idea of ditching the stone in the sand, to be reclaimed by the elements, seemed the decent thing to do.

But Andrea was not to be deterred. "It needn't be so daunting," she said. "If what your father told you is correct, certain facts are key. Most obvious: Ayers Rock as the source, then that he found the stone in a *camel's* saddlebag. Begin with that. Camels were used for inland exploration only after 1860. Ayers Rock wasn't found until 1872. Tjurunga are not directly noted in the literature until…a vague reference in 1875…. In 1877, there was a tjurunga theft by Giles, but that was in the Great Victorian Desert. Let's see, Centralian routes past the Rock to Hermannsburg…Long shots discounted, that takes us up to the 1890s and the Horn Scientific Expedition."

She named Baldwin Spencer.

"I know he traveled that route on the Horn. And he became an avid collector of tjurunga. With an hour well spent, you could at least eliminate him as a candidate. Read the expedition report and you'll know. And you'd also know which clans he came in contact with. After that, you need only hand over the stone to the appropriate Land Council.

There was still an entire afternoon ahead of me. I would look at the Horn Expedition's Report if she requisitioned it for me. All I had to do was wait for my book in the reading room down on the first floor.

She opened her door to show me out and stood there looking at me, rather sternly. "There are people on our staff who have sensitivities. Just please wait and keep to yourself."

The Jubilee Reading Room is a small sanctum, an intimate paneled chamber heralded in gold-leaf "Historical Treasures." Inside, the atmosphere was saturated with light filtered through tall arched windows, and two stout tables hosted researchers laboring in the stillness and the silence. I lay down my satchel and sat at a table with a view of the door through which my book would arrive. I laid out the Moleskine and a pencil. I waited. I toyed with the brass pull chain of the table's reading light, letting it drape over my finger and fall twitching like a puppy's tail, catching the window light in little flashes. The desk librarian received a trolley of materials and forwarded it to another's table.

Then the still and the quiet returned, now intensified. Back home, it was the middle of the night. I folded my hands together on the desk and laid down my head.

I woke to the muffled sound of reggae from behind a book trolley parked at my table, the material piled so high that I only glimpsed the Rasta beanie – red, yellow, green – gliding away. Andrea, the librarian, had insanely oversupplied my interest.

Before me was stacked more than a hundred years of expedition logs both originals and in facsimile, scrawled letters in binders, and reports ranging back to Australia's earliest geographic explorations. There were transcripts of addresses given to the accompaniment of lantern slides in Great Britain by credentialed men whose surnames were followed with M.D.s, M.A.s, D.Sc.s, M.I.E.s and F.R.S.s. And there were proceedings from the Royal Geographic Society of Australasia whose meetings were punctuated with "cheers" and "applause." Up until 1840, Australia's interior was entirely unknown, an "untrodden wilderness" that provided an explorer the opportunity to rank his resolve and grit against the glory everywhere attending the British flag, to earn his leaf in the laurel crown of English exploration.

These reports told of journeys across impossible terrain. It was a land described by Colonel Peter Egerton Warburton as "the greatest absolute blank on the face of the globe–the polar regions excepted… barren and inhospitable–a dreary waste, a howling wilderness," all this writ "whilst the agony was fresh in mind."

Hours hence, when the desk librarian advised me that the day was nearly over, I had dallied too long just for the pleasure of Victorian prose and had made only random notes. I begged a little more time to read the material Andrea most wanted me to examine, the 1894 Report of the Horn Scientific Expedition, represented by two fat volumes.

I unfolded the map that hinged off a front cover and traced the dashed route line. The expedition's trail did indeed lead to Ayers Rock and thence to the Lutheran mission at Hermannsburg, the site where my father acquired his tjurunga stone.

And here was Baldwin Spencer, the naturalist on the Horn, atop his camel, the Baron:

> Perched up high between heaven and earth, you may
> often see, say, a lizard or insect which you are anxious to
> secure, but long before you can persuade your camel to
> sit down the [lizard] is far away and safely hidden. The
> chances are, too, that you return from a fruitless search
> to find that your camel, which above all things dislikes to
> be left behind its companions, has trotted away.

Had Baron been the accomplice whose saddlebags had carried off my father's pilfered stone? Not up to this point.

The Horn Expedition was en route to Ayers Rock. But just before reaching it, the party had split in two and one of the groups headed directly to a place called Haasts Bluff. While Spencer was at the "Rock" digging up honey ants and describing their habits, Mr. Horn and the expedition's surveyor Charles Winnecke were cajoling one of their Aboriginal guides, dubbed Racehorse, to lead them to a particular cave.

I copied out Dr. Philip Jones's more recent historical account, his libretto of the tjurunga heist, in his *Objects of Mystery and Concealment*.

According to Winnecke, the existence of the site had been known to Europeans for some time.

> 'Many expeditions have started in search of this cave,
> but hitherto all have failed to find it as nothing would
> induce the local natives to betray its whereabouts. ...I...
> elicited the information that a large number of corroboree
> stones [tjurunga] were hidden in a cave in the ranges to
> the eastward...' (Winnecke 1897: 42)

> Of the...fifteen incised stones in the cave, Stirling and
> Winnecke removed [them all], substituting 'tomahawks,
> large knives, and other things in their place, sufficient
> commercially to make the transaction an equitable
> exchange.' (Ibid.)

That the robbery was going to cost a life did not occur, or didn't matter, to Winnecke. Dr. Jones quotes this fragment of a letter to him from the Outback telegrapher Frank Gillen.

'I hear that Racehorse has had to seek permanent police protection through showing your party where those chooringa [sic] (which you ruthlessly robbed!!) were deposited.' (13 October, 1894)

Four decades later, Theodore Strehlow, making his debut in the Centre as an ethnologist, found that the fate of Racehorse was still being discussed. Strehlow's Aboriginal informant told him that the Horn Expedition's native guide had been ritually executed – stood up and speared by his fellows – for his betrayal of their sacred cave's whereabouts.

For all the grief sowed, Mr. Horn could say pitifully little about his stolen tjurunga, only that "special value was attached to them," that "they had some kind of connection with important rites and ceremonies."

My father's assertion, that his stone had a pirate's pedigree, had proven to be at least plausible. But no report told of Baldwin Spencer or anyone else from any of the other expeditions having plundered Ayers Rock. I was further from securing a home for it than when I'd started out this morning. In the Jubilee Room, with its increasingly fading light, my day had been long, my eyes worn down, and my bottom was sore. My goal now was for Allen to get me to his house and into a glass of wine as quickly as possible.

（7）

ALLEN HAD TOLD ME where to find him after his last class of the day, on a building's fourth-floor level. Waiting for him to finish up, I stood against the corridor window, my eyes wandering across the adjacent parkland and along the bows of River Torrens's course. Right there, on my eleventh birthday, my father had launched me into that very bend in a rented rowboat. The flowing of the Torrens brought me back to shore. Dad's shoe gave a shove to my stern; it sent me adrift with oars all amuck. It was the only help I got from him, a push into the current. Chuckling to himself, he retired to a bench while I zigzagged up the stream, careening off the banks toward an uncertain goal.

A bell rang, doors flew open, and students, released for the weekend, poured out.

Allen and I walked to the elevator accompanied by his graduate assistant Peter – short-legged, with tufts of hair projecting from under his T-shirt and around the thongs of his sandals. Wild, frizzy hair everywhere. Previously, Peter had run a guerrilla theater troupe in the streets of Johannesburg. Denied admission to the university's theater department, he had switched to anthropology and not looked back. Allen strode ahead of us, nodding regally to students, as I babbled to Peter about the lessons and frustrations of my day. He was not surprised.

I asked him, "What happened to the tjurunga stolen by the Horn Expedition?"

"You know about that? Good on ya."

"1896. The leader gutted a sacred cave and left behind trade goods." I wanted to know what had become of the native men and their stolen sacra. Was any restitution ever made to their descendants or did memory of the episode simply fade away?

"Just four years ago, seventy-five years after the incident, an anthropologist with a wooden crate in the boot of his Land Cruiser drove away from Alice Springs, down a long sand road through what is now a national park, and beyond into Aboriginal freehold to the community at Haasts Bluff, the scene of the original crime. He left the crate there, with the land's traditional owners, and the tjurunga stones departed forever from white control or public concern. You can take some encouragement from that, I suppose."

Provoked by a sudden thought, Peter said, "You should take your stone to Alice Springs." I laughed. I thought it was a joke.

"There's a Rock Art Congress meeting in Alice. It begins in a couple of days," he continued. "I'll get you the name of the director."

"A tjurunga is rock art?"

"No. It's just that these people necessarily have a lot to do with the local Aboriginal landowners. Might be a useful connection for you there."

He unpinned a Rock Art Association flyer from Allen's office corkboard and both men – Allen rather skeptically – watched as I dialed Melbourne. Murray, the conference chair, answered the phone. I introduced myself and explained my dilemma.

Murray patiently heard me out, then responded with what sounded like a coherent plan. He said that several Aboriginal leaders would be attending the three-day Congress. Why settle for making inquiries, he suggested, when the Congress itself would be an ideal venue for a "hand back" of the tjurunga. He insisted, "Yes, indeed, do come. I'll make it work."

As quickly as that, my next call was to reserve a berth on the first train to Alice Springs, an overnighter leaving Adelaide at noon tomorrow. I jumped up and gave Peter a hearty handshake.

At Allen's house, the family circus was again in full swing. Awaiting dinner we two settled ourselves on a sofa with glasses of wine. I told him how I had kept running into the name Strehlow, Strehlow, Theodore Strehlow, and that I'd come within ten feet of his book *Songs of Central Australia.*

"Interesting chap, Strehlow. He affected every aspect of Aboriginal/white relations: the way we deal with each other personally and legally, how sacred objects and secret information are handled, the shape of anthropology in Australia, and on and on. He died the most celebrated and the most vilified ethnologist in our history. A renowned collector. Left behind yards and yards of tjurunga."

"Tell me more."

Allen stood and stepped to his bar with our glasses, pouring a measure for each of us. "For a while, bands of natives were coming out from the desert to see Strehlow, looking for their fathers' tjurunga. They told him, 'The sacred ways have to be carried on.' Strehlow stood his ground, though. He demanded, 'Then sing your sacred songs as they were given to you by your father or grandfather.' Of course he knew the songs better than they did. In the end, he just told them to mind their own business."

I offered, "Bruce Chatwin calls Strehlow 'a bit of a cuss.' "

"At the peak of the tussle Strehlow was preparing for the opening event of the foundation that would carry on his life's work. Distraught on the night before he died, he wrote a final entry in his diary: two swans, the decoration on the party cake, had broken off in the delivery car."

"*Cake?* What about the tjurunga?"

"Well, that's the problem, isn't it? When the Old Man died, everyone wanted into his treasure room. Early on, Strehlow had named his infant son Carl as heir to everything he'd collected. So then, the whole kit and caboodle went to Carl, who was now grown. All too much for *his* interest. He put a good lot of them up at auction. Of course, that reached the attention of native men in the Centre, the erstwhile heirs of *their* fathers' sacred objects. They really wanted their stuff back."

Allen brought the bottle of wine to our sofa. Anya quickly came over and snatched it back. She emptied the bottle's last pour into her glass, stuck her tongue out at us, and returned to the kitchen. "Alarms are sounded. There are more forays by men from the desert. The Land Council in Alice Springs is howling, and the activists are running hot. By now, you see, the Strehlow collection in its entirety was known as the 'Crown Jewels of Australia.' Then the infamous raid – Strehlow's house ransacked by the State. It was a chilling reenactment..."

"Of Horn's raid on the cave. I can see that."

"The agents gathered up everything. Carted it all away. Left behind a receipt."

"Daddy. Come," Caitlin called out. Allen stood up, and I stood with him for the conclusion. "All the tjurunga are placed in the museum's vault. Meanwhile, negotiations are underway with Carl and Strehlow's widow over the terms of the collection's future. Offers are made and rejected. The government eventually proposes that a new institution be built in Alice Springs to house everything. They call it the Strehlow Research Centre. It's there now, and it follows the wishes of the Old Man as expressed in his lifetime. In other words, now that the tjurunga are in the SRC, shielded by old Strehlow's wishes, they will never come out again, can never be returned to Aboriginal communities."

Allen's office was not laid out for entertaining. He sat behind a gray government-surplus desk piled with papers and books, all flagged with yellow slips. On one wall hung a large map that showed the distribution of native language groups in Australia's central deserts and behind his desk was a gaudily colored Aboriginal dot painting that he had brought out of the desert a decade before. My satchel lay beside the door, the stone perched upright like a dog eager for her walk.

"You know," I said in Allen's direction, "I'm not the first guy to do this." That is, to accompany home tjurunga that had been collected by his father. Allen, at his desk, remained head down studying something, fingers drumming the desktop.

Simon Pockley had passed through Adelaide four years earlier. I knew him from our correspondence. He was a Ph.D. candidate, and I had read his thesis, which was posted online. It included an account of his heading into the Centre with tjurunga inherited from his father, Dr. John Pockley. His father had been part of a 1933 physiological research expedition intending to measure how Aboriginals "won their awesome battle to survive in a cruel environment." According to the diary Dr. Pockley kept, he had talked his way onto the expedition team with "gin lubrication" and a promise to "share any booty in the way of churingas [sic]" with his fellows. Of the eleven objects he managed to acquire, seven were passed down to his son Simon.

Sixty years after their removal, Simon carried those seven back into the Centre. He explained his reasons to me in an email: "Perhaps it is simply that this collection is part of my own cultural memory. Perhaps it is the journey of the son around the father."

Within days of his arrival at the Centre, Pockley turned around and went back home carrying all the items he had intended to leave behind. "What I discovered was a seething can of worms in which political and personal agendas prevail." The return of my own father's tjurunga was better plotted. Murray, the Rock Art Congress chair, knew his way around.

Allen closed his laptop, eased back from the desk, and brandished his wristwatch. "Ready?"

On our way to the station, he was sullen. "You know you're not going to find someone walking halfway across the conference stage to meet you and muttering to himself, 'Damn. I should never have sold that thing to a tourist in the sixties. Why did I do that?' And, 'Ah, here comes his son. Let's have a look at what he's got.' You know it can't be that easy."

His words were no more to me than a passing breeze. By now I had seen a photograph of Theodore Strehlow's face as a young man, the "foolish romantic," the "puck of the desert," as he first saddled his camels to embark upon his career at the Centre, all boyish charm and good looks. Of Chatwin, I knew little more than his prancing prose and what the roguish book-jacket photo could suggest. But I already felt like I was somehow traveling between the two of them, buoyed up between their unequal shoulders. It would have been nice to have Allen's endorsement, too, but he was not in the mood.

"Poor sod," said Allen. "I can see it. You've got stars in your eyes. And you're about to have them punched."

(8)

T HE ADELAIDE HILLS slipped away, and coastal fog banks that had swirled around us yielded to dense gray clouds overhead. They hung over field after field after field of farmers' land. A succession of rainbows burst from distant showers, mile after mile, the brilliant arcs dipping into the earth seemingly to emerge once again, arcing up and turning back into the earth like some headless serpent leading us along our course. Outstripping the last degree of humidity as though through speed, we dieseled into the Big Dry.

With my books, the Moleskine, and a flask, I made my way inside the Vista Car to settle in. Most of the benches were piled with children doubled up for sleep, little black arms and white legs draped every which way. They were in the care of two black matrons and a younger white woman whose periwinkle blue sundress lay loosely against her russet-colored bosom, a sleeping Aboriginal child draped across her lap. I dropped into the empty seat opposite her. She would be these kids' teacher at a settlement school or an orphanage somewhere further up is what I thought.

She had a little sideways bend in the bridge of her nose, and her long hair was uncombed and not quite dry. Sea salt crystals sparkled around her eyes. She acknowledged my gaze and smiled. I asked if she was returning from a trip to the ocean, "the Big Wet," I said, eager to make conversation with a dinkum Centralian.

She asked me, "First time out?" and I nodded. She returned the nod, then added, "In the Centre you can go for years without seeing a cloud. My youngest brother was four when it rained for the first time in his life. It was night and it terrified him, this drumming on the sheet metal roof over our beds. He had no idea what it was." She turned to her window where the Adelaide hills had fallen from view and said, "What a marvelous thing it is to see a cloud. And when a spot of shade comes over you softening the heat, can you imagine, it's a remarkable feeling. Like a supernatural event."

Remarkable, yes. I felt that I wasn't so much *going* to the Centre as being *drawn* there, out of the mundane and into the super natural. Everything around me seemed like a miracle: our speed, those children, the dusk descending. I wanted to embrace it all. If only I could lead this woman to my berth and lift off her skirt, I would caress her body with my mouth, softly as the shadow of a cloud. She looked down at the child whose head she stroked, smiled to herself and closed her eyes.

That Night I went to sleep studying the complementary route map that highlighted what there was to see, very little actually, along our ruler-straight path into Northern Territory. It advises the reader to look for "the world's oldest continually running course," the Finke River. I woke next morning just in time to witness our crossing of this waterway. A few trees stood along the shallow gully, but the water was not running. Everything else, as far as I could see toward the horizon, appeared barren, choked by heat.

Sometime during the night our train had crossed the latitude of Cooper Creek. Once before I had come just this far into the interior, with Dad, one day's drive in his Land Rover from Adelaide. He was taking me to visit his work camp. There, as we would see, a horde of men labored in khaki shorts and unlaced boots, brutishly disturbing the earth's subsurface with their explosives.

En route to camp, we stopped at Cooper Creek, at the area where the explorers Robert Burke and John Wills met their deaths in 1861. Dad took a photograph, posing me next to a pile of withered wreaths heaped against a stone monument. The slide is overexposed, bleached white except in the shadows where some sparse color persists. I am twelve years old, my pants are riding high, and a gray plastic Brownie Hawkeye hangs by a strap around my neck.

The Burke and Wills expedition's goal, a continental traverse, had commenced with festive trumpets blowing. It ended somberly, with mythic status granted to the fallen. The Melbourne *Age* had reported, "The entire company of explorers has been dissipated out of being, like dewdrops before the sun." Romantic images of Burke and Wills were rushed into art and poetry, memorializing them as national heroes who had engaged a worthy but indomitable foe, the Australian desert.

It has been said that the frightful deaths of Burke and Wills, their martyrdom to the land, bought the colony full rights to everything therein. The brutality of the colonial frontier followed them to Cooper Creek and, by the turn of the century, had passed northward like a fever. My father's prospecting for oil was beholden to them in the same way as the sequential waves of explorers, drovers, squatters, miners and missionaries before him.

The door of Dad's field-office trailer slammed closed behind us. The flies outside, undisturbed, clung to the screen. I had never seen my father like this, so in his element and twice the size I knew. At home, fresh from the field or soon to return, he would unroll his maps over our dinner table, spending hours leaning into them. Here on the trailer wall, he had taped up one of those maps, all geomorphic contours with their naturally sinuous lines. He had drawn his own quadrangular grid over all of it. With extraction foremost on his mind, he'd placed a red pin for every shot-point his crew would make in the field, a dozen to a row, row upon row.

Now he drives me out for a look, to see his men at their jobs. All his trucks are special-built, the drill truck fitted with a derrick standing erect at its rear. It humps the earth, lifting and vibrating as it bores shafts for the explosive charges. A man is laying seismophones on the ground exactly where the map says they should be. "Like stethoscopes," the man says to me as he unspools a cable. He points to his chest. "It's how we know what's ticking inside." One stick of dynamite is slid down each hole, the fuse wires joined into a single strand and run to the fire-box.

Twelve geysers of sand shoot up at once. As the dust settles, no one moves while shock waves travel deep into the earth. Layer after layer of strata return a distinctive echo to the surface where the phones catch them. Inside the truck, twelve twitching needles lay ink lines side by side down a long paper tape; twelve vibrations whose variances, the recording crewman tells me, no man can better read than my father.

Dad has brought me into his world and his men are giving me the respect that is due to their chief. I love my Dad so much right now.

I imagine that my father feels the same way toward me, that he wants to tell me that he loves me, or intends to tell me at some point. Inside the recording truck, he pulls the tape from its collecting basket and sits with it on the running board. To his twelve-year-old son, this is how it is: "Look at these refraction traces. It's a thick Permian section. See this buckle in the rock plate? That could contain gas-cut salt water or it might be oil. Could be oil, or gas, or it might be nothing of use to me."

9

THE RUST-COLORED Macdonnell Ranges, the first topographic relief since Adelaide, rose up before us, stretching left and right to disappear at the horizons in a pristine blue tinge. We flashed past groves of date palm set precisely in rows like the arched columns of an Andalusian mosque. Then a blacktopped roadway appeared out of the scrub and drew alongside the train's track, quickly to be joined by the dry bed of the Todd River. All three courses streamed together for the final half-mile toward Alice Springs.

The train slowed into Heavitree Gap, a cleavage in the MacDonnells, preparing to brake at the terminal. Aboriginal adults ambled along the siding, and from the Todd's sand bed their children waved up to our train as we slid past. These families, arriving in town for hospital visits or football festivals, claimed the accommodating Todd for their hotel. They come from three abutting states and several linguistic groups, including Anmatjera, Kaitija, Walbiri, Pintubi, Pitjantjatjara, Warramunga, and the Aranda, which alone comprises ten distinct dialects, altogether making Alice Springs the most cosmopolitan native town in the country.

Alice Springs's reputation for isolation draws hundreds of thousands of fly-in tourists every year. In a couple of days, I would be flying out of Alice, easting to Cairns and the Great Barrier Reef. I had paid more than I thought possible for a yellow silicone mask and pair of flippers. I could almost smell the salt-tanged air.

The schoolteacher in her periwinkle blue dress, her companions, and their charges crowded around me at the train's door. Would I ever see her again? I ducked below her hat's wide brim. "Where's home?"

"Not here," she answered.

"What other places are there?"

"Utopia. We live in Utopia." She said this with a straight face, then spoke in an Aboriginal tongue to one of the black women who were with her. They looked me up and down and, laughing, stepped off the train. The engine let out a sigh.

Passengers poured onto the platform while, for a moment longer, I remained aboard to survey the terrain. Over the station roof, my sight easily reached the bordering Ranges. From their low summit one might look down on the town in full, divided by the dry Todd with its dozens of paisley-shaped islets.

There was something very familiar about the place.

No one I knew, other than my father, had been to Alice Springs and I certainly had not. Neither did the town merit wordy portrayal in anything I had read, although two British writers came easily to mind. Chatwin disposed of Alice Springs in a single sentence: "a grid of scorching streets where men in long white socks were forever getting in and out of Land Cruisers." And Nevil Shute gave it a fanciful aura in *A Town Like Alice*, writing that it gave off "a faint suggestion of an English suburb" where the women "spoke quite naturally of England as 'home' though none of them had ever been there."

That – Australia's devotion to England, and its monarchy – triggered the scene I was reaching for.

My father, on his way to a work site, had arrived in Alice Springs at the same time as Queen Elizabeth, and found himself in a position to snap a couple of photos along the Royal pathway. In one picture I can see over the Queen's white Breton hat, toward the orange hills beyond, the whole town nearly end to end.

Just days before that picture was taken, I myself had seen the Queen, watching her advance down Adelaide's King William Street in a mirror-polished Rolls Royce. In Dad's Alice Springs photo she is riding an open-top Land Rover, her personal flag snapping above the drab green hood. She is ungloved, and Phillip, who has shed his jacket, waves to the left and the right; they are allowing themselves to be adored. At the Old Timers' Home, several pioneers had gathered under a banner offering, "Welcome to Her Majesty." But because there was no native word for "monarch," Aboriginal children on the wayside shouted at the motorcade, "Kangkintjai!" which optimistically translates as "welcome beloved."

Instead of starched Police Lancers who had preceded her on parade through Adelaide, mounted on uniformly magnificent steeds, in Alice Springs the local Pony Club accompanied her to the fairground. Here a shaded platform awaited the Royal Couple. Dad's last photo was of two stockmen under broad felt hats rising up off their heels at the rail fence, their pint-sized sons standing alongside in shorts and little bush hats. As the Queen glides by the youngsters, they appear frozen with awe. Each grips an Aussie flag: the constellation of the Southern Cross on a field of midnight blue, Britain's Union Jack blazing from one corner.

The thirty-seven-year-old monarch had come to see for herself, two hundred years after it began, the remains of Great Britain's last colonial experiment. She arrived in Central Australia thinking of it as the fringe of the Empire. Now she was seeing into its heart, even though the racial turmoil that defines Alice Springs was, for the Queen's Day, as subdued as any act of courtly etiquette.

From the fairground platform, offering some benign remarks for relations between the citizens and the Aboriginals, Her Royal Highness began a short address: "There are very few areas in the world which give rise to such conflicting feelings as this Northern Territory."

At the center of a very thirsty continent, the Alice stands both for utter isolation and relief. The town floats mirage-like on its beer, not as Nevil Shute put it, on milkbar ice cream sodas. But Shute was factual on one account: monarchial mystification does indeed haunt Alice Springs. Elizabeth and Philip were put up that night in the territory governor's Residency, which is now a museum. The porcelain commode that the Queen sat upon, on which by propriety no one else might henceforth sit, is recalled only by its ghostly outline on the bathroom's tile floor, a trace of what she left behind.

With the stone-heavy satchel over my shoulder, I tugged my duffel onto the platform. I also cradled a pillowcase of souvenirs pilfered from the train: my dinner plate, a teacup, an ashtray and most anything at hand that was blazoned with the train's logo, a red camel's head. I reckoned my theft a fair exchange on the cosmic balance sheet for Dad's tjurunga stone, to be given up at tomorrow's Rock Art Congress.

The platform was empty but for three Aboriginals who, I was sure, had not been onboard. There they stood, two car lengths away, perfectly still, looking in my direction and apparently waiting for me. In an instant, I knew they sensed what I was carrying. Clutching more firmly the tjurunga, I began to skirt around them.

I scrutinized them, if obliquely, with the same intensity they fixed on me. The woman was the tiniest adult I had ever seen, almost lost in her grab-bag dress, an outsized vinyl purse hanging high across her chest. She stood deferentially several feet behind the two men and gazed blankly away, although her eyes occasionally fluttered in apparent surprise at nothing in particular.

Taller than her by only six inches to the top of his sweat-stained hat, her nearest companion exhaled clouds of tobacco smoke across his full jowls, a buckle suspending his belly well in front of him, and a nearly empty plastic Coke bottle dangled from his fingertips.

The third, standing ahead of the others, had a morbidly intense demeanor. Older, his chest bare and with muscles taut across his black torso, he wore a bright red sweatband; it pulled his hair back very harshly to expose a plucked and burnished forehead. I noticed little else besides the intensity of his gaze. And as I came abreast this man, he spoke to me in a flat voice.

He may have asked, "You got anything for me?" But what I heard was, "You are the courier we have been waiting for. I'll take the tjurunga from here." Streamers of sweat slid down from my armpits.

How could I give up so easily what my father had safeguarded for thirty years? Should I explain to him that what I carried was already promised? What would I say to Murray, the conference chair, who had planned a ceremonial on-stage hand over – that "I gave it away to the first person I met, a stranger at the train station?"

As a guest in Aboriginal country, I did not want to be unchari-table, or worse, to *offend*. In my right hand was the white pillowcase embroidered with the train's logo. The china clinked as I lifted it up to him. The woman stepped forward, took the bag and the three of them left. They simply turned, walked off the platform and across the tracks.

A cabbie, arriving late to the station and hoping for a last fare, found me standing on the platform, just arrived and already out of my depth. He took my duffel bag and led me away.

Mid-block on a strip facing the town Green, which was not green but rather like parchment, and opposite the Public Library, the Desert Bookstore presented its weathered storefront. In its plate window a digital clock was holding at 45,000 years, adjustable backward when-ever an archaeologist reset the antiquity of Aboriginal Australia. The interior, long and narrow, grew dimmer and cooler as it receded toward Enid Lacey's cluttered desk that was pushed against a wall of books. At the store's farthest reach she kept artists' supplies – rolls of canvas, tubes of paint and jars of brushes – and hung a few paintings close to the ceiling although it had been a long time since her bookstore was the town's main gallery. The new art enterprises on the pedestrian mall had glitz; planted against each window was a forest of didgeridoos and racks of boomerangs all brightly painted to catch the eye, draw in "the bloody toorists," and turn out their pockets.

Chatwin, in the opening scene of *Songlines*, describes the proprietor of the Desert Bookstore as having "lived with Aboriginals all her life. She had almost every book about Central Australia and tried to stock every title in print." Enid had aged fifteen years past meeting Chatwin, her nose and chin no doubt were sharper than they were, and her hair let go a natural gray. But the same two pair of glasses on their chains still dangled from around her neck. I sat where she told me to wait, on "Chatwin's throne," a high-backed wicker chair with a sunken seat from which he had once held court. The author was at the peak of his powers and contemplating his most daunting subject, the Aboriginal Dreamtime. I saw in front of me a scene Chatwin might himself have described: a hulking Aboriginal man who could find no place to hide from Enid. She held the painting he had made the mistake of offering her.

"You haven't done what I told you to do, Philip. Please take it away."

The small, unframed canvas was, I thought, a pretty and very saleable desert landscape with all the iconic elements in place: a dry riverbed, a stout yet sinuous gum tree, and the red rock hills. Philip, whose musty body perfume filled the room, stood wringing his hands and muttering into his chest.

"It's not finished, and I'm not going to give you drinking money for a painting that I cannot sell. Now be off with you!" Her practiced fulmination concluded, Philip rejoined his pals who were waiting on the sidewalk.

Enid and I were alone in the store. I asked about Philip and his friends who looked a bit down on their luck. Chatwin had summarized a hundred years of social programs aimed at improving the natives' lot with, "What could be done for the Aboriginals was to preserve their most essential liberty: the liberty to remain poor." I put that to Enid.

"Bruce was the one sentence wonder, wasn't he?"

"A century ago this would've been tribal land," I said.

"This is Aranda land, traditionally. The Aranda allot river sections to the other groups. Their sacred sites need looking after, too."

"Still? Sacred sites?"

"Oh, they're here," she sang out. "Your train passed right through one in the MacDonnells. That's a Caterpillar Dreaming. Lost his tail to dynamite, bulldozed for access to the casino. Just up a bit, Emily Gap is a major site. Picnic spot as well, defaced by vandals. And over that way is Pine Gap. Or *was*. A military base now."

Enid asked why I was in town. I told her all about my father and his stone, about the unproven story of its source and tomorrow's ceremonial return. "So," I asked, "have you got anything on Aboriginal sacred objects?" She hesitated a moment, then stepped from around her desk. She signaled for me to follow.

Her stock room was a tidy alcove that just afforded space for a teakettle, above which was a shelf that held her small private library. She pulled a hefty volume down onto the counter, Charles Mountford's 1976 *Nomads of the Australian Desert*.

"You might find something useful in here," Enid said. It was an encyclopedia of sacred knowledge that initiates once paid dearly to learn and suddenly that knowledge could be purchased in a bookstore for just a few dollars.

The author, she said, went to press even as Aboriginal awareness about the dangers of losing control of their secret/sacred learning was becoming more keenly felt. Mountford, with his first words in *Nomads*, cautioned his readers: "The concept of what is secret in Aboriginal religious belief and action must on all occasions be observed." The old men had willingly shared their secrets with the white scholar who then disregarded his own advice. His caution, which he printed on the flyleaf, became evidence entered against him in court when summoned for breach of contract.

By court order, *Nomads* had been forced off the shelves of bookstores throughout Northern Territory, and all the copies were trucked back to the publisher in Sydney. "They were remaindered at five dollars," Enid said. She was still fuming over what she saw as censorship and, not surprisingly, an infringement on her business.

"They had no right," she said. "Poor Monty. Political go-getters ruined a sterling career."

Shelving the tome, she said, "You can't have this one. But read *Nomads* and also Strehlow's *Aranda Traditions*. They're both across the Green. Special Collections."

At the rear of the Nevil Shute Public Library, three Aboriginal boys were huddled in front of a video screen watching a Western, the circled wagon scene. They pounded each other on the back and laughed hysterically as one after another Wild Indian, getting shot, came tumbling backward off his horse. Behind them was the glass wall of Special Collections. The door opened as I approached and quickly swept closed again behind me. Inside was the smell of lilacs. Sissy Martin, archivist to a dense collection of Centralian history, law, and philosophy, met my approach with raised eyebrows. She wore a sleeveless cotton blouse in a peony print. In addition to a rack of the pamphlet *Arid Lands Gardening*, she kept taped to her desk a sign-up sheet for the community's weekend bush trek, both hobbies accounting for her slender, sun-kissed arms.

Sissy heard me out. She cleared a table and pulled down books selected for their references to tjurunga, then stayed past hours as I plugged my dollar coins by the handfuls into her copy machine.

In *Nomads of the Australian Desert*, I found that Mountford depicts tjurunga as "a concentrated mass of life essence," as though the stone might be a body's vital organ. Was that what the mystic on the train platform heard, a faint drumming coming from inside my satchel? Then anthropologist Nancy Munn, in her essay *Transformation of Subjects into Objects*, estimates tjurunga as a "particular form or mode of experiencing the world in which symbols of collectivity are constantly recharged with intimations of self." Reading Munn made my head spin. The Alice Springs historian Richard Kimber wrote that tjurunga were like "compressed chunks of meaning and of power and of knowledge about the entire cosmos and how people fit into it." Nothing yet in my tjurunga came close to matching those qualities. And Géza Róheim dismembers the very word to reveal that *tju-* translates as *shame* and *–runga* means *one's own*, and so concluded that "tjurunga (penis) has something to do with shame and with…coming into being." Sex, I thought. *Someone* at least is telling the truth. Taking a more literary tack, David Abram claims that a tjurunga is like "the Kabbalah, the esoteric body of Jewish mysticism…a magic gateway or guide into an entire sphere of existence."

I felt numb with all this abstract "talk," but still there was more. Near the bottom of the pile was *The Savage Mind*. I laughed out loud, a little loopy with fatigue, at the fellow's box-stepping hyperbole: "Sissy, what on earth does this mean? A tjurunga: 'The diachronic essence of diachrony at the very heart of synchrony.' "

"Lévi-Strauss," she said picking up the books that I had finished going through. "What you just read, that would be the gold standard for a structural anthropologist."

"Well, fine," I sighed, handing him over. "It's all *open to interpretation*. But where do they get this stuff?"

Replacing my books onto the shelves, one here, one there, Sissy said, "He 'did not find sermons in stones. He had the sermons already; his task was to find the stones to fit them.' Brownell on Hawthorne."

"I suppose it doesn't do any harm, not to a tjurunga," I said. "Crusty surface but – Hey! Limitless depth."

"Are we about done here, Mark?"

There was a single book left to deal with, one by a man who sympathetically summoned the Aboriginal experience – Theodore Strehlow. Fanning the pages, stopping randomly, I read that each tjurunga is the immortal body of a totemic ancestor, transformed at the end of its primordial labors. The old bear himself provided an excellent reason to help a tjurunga home, and not just into a thesis: Every tjurunga is a living man's eternal father. It's about one's obligation to father.

His book *Aranda Traditions* was the last to pass through the copier and the reason I kept Sissy past closing time. That evening, Strehlow's were the pages that I read while balanced on a bar stool at the saloon across the street.

The Victoria Bitter could not, in any quantity, calm my excitement with *Aranda Traditions* and its panoramic view of the Arandic sacred life. Introducing his Aranda subjects, Theodore Strehlow coyly conceded their "amazing heritage of an age-old native culture of no mean order."

Strehlow began his research in 1932 when the grasp of "white intruders" was still early. Diagramed on the book's frontispiece map, cattle stations are overwhelmed within overlapping, amoeba-shaped Aranda estates. Each of these estates hosted one or more sanctuaries replete with its tjurunga objects. I took a deep draw from the chocolate-colored brew, uncapped my highlighter and stepped with Strehlow back three-quarters of a century, into the province of manhood and myth.

Strehlow was an impassioned observer, so his accounts, while exacting, are also emotionally charged. He presents a young Aranda man anticipating the privileges of manhood, facing the ordeals of his initiation with "eager expectation and with a cheerful courage that sustains him more or less successfully in the hour of trial." The initiate would receive his share of sacred knowledge and be charged with the responsibility of looking after it; this was his clan's heritage. He will soon be taken to the tjurunga cave for a first viewing of the objects on whose maintenance the perpetuation of all life depends.

"The cave must be approached with awe and reverence... for to disturb the ancestral spirits rudely means to court their displeasure, and this may result in a sudden death." The Elders, having announced themselves by tossing ahead bits of stick and stone, escort the initiate into the vicinity of the storehouse. Through hand signals, the boy is shown evidence of the ancestors' presence.

The sacred objects are found "massed together, heavily red-ochred and bound together into a number of separate bundles by means of hair-string made from human hair." The men lay down everything they brought with them and "at a sign from the leader, the party sits down in a half-circle." As one man advances to remove the tjurunga from their resting place, the others begin to chant verses from the totemic ancestor's sacred songs.

"In low hushed voices their song bursts upon the silence that has enfolded the cave up to this moment...and the song re-echoes from the steep mountain wall. It is upon this old traditional chant, the words of which are jealously guarded by the old men of the group, that the whole of the myth is based." And just as I was reading this, I thought I could hear my grandfather Reverend Marcus's treadle organ.

I once had a photo of him on the bed of a truck, working the keyboard and bellows. The device was a collapsible affair that he carted around to camp meetings, the bellows concealed by tattered burgundy brocade. He would sing, "There is a river pure and bright, whose streams make glad the heavenly." When did I lose track of his hymnal, its loosened pages bound with twisted cord and wrapped all round with waterproofing? I drained my glass and signaled the barkeep for another draw.

Returning to the cave, I see that the hair strings have been unwound from the tjurunga. The stones are now passed among the men who press them each "affectionately to his body." The initiate is handed the tjurunga along with a first exposure to the relevant myth of which, as he proves himself worthy, he will eventually acquire complete knowledge.

I do *still* have one of Grandfather's notebooks. It is filled with contempt for Sigmund Freud, whose every claim the Reverend believed he had rebutted point for point.

On taboo, when Freud assigned its beginnings to *primitive culture*, a relic preserved in our subconscious, Marcus countered that God's command to Adam was the original taboo, devised especially for his weakness, both taboo and weakness communicated forward. Freud made his case emphatically by citing the Aboriginal Australian, while my grandfather battled forth with the Old Testament in hand.

"The possession of the sacred objects," continues Strehlow, "brings with it the ownership of the legend, the chant, and the ceremonies associated with them." The stone's custodian is responsible both to his own clan and to the network of distant clans across whose estates his totemic ancestor had wandered long ago.

An initiate's assignment of tribal values is, I knew, an age-old drama whether conducted in a dark cave or consummated on stage with an Eagle Scout sash. And the consequences of indoctrination vary just as widely. While I could leave my grandfather's central Texas "estate" with hardly a look back, Strehlow's Aranda youth were "firmly fettered by the rigid bonds of their tradition." The paramount privilege of Arandic manhood was to regularly perform the rituals that called forth the ancestor's good will. But that, of course, was then.

Strehlow had begun his ethnological work in Central Australia at the onset of decline in the Aranda's traditional religious knowledge; the Elders were already beginning to despair. Although the caves still concealed their tjurunga, the Elders were having trouble keeping the faith alive. Not only were there devastating droughts, introduced influenza and the constables with their black trackers, all of which left human corpses scattered in the desert, there were also sons who would someday fail their fathers.

Strehlow quotes Wutupia, a gray-beard: "I am a member of the younger generation. I was always working for the white man. I was not judged worthy to be entrusted with the verses. I am wholly ignorant, just like a white man."

My glass was empty. The watchful barman brought another.

My grandfather's rural church in Texas. It was a child's drawing of a big house – peaked roof, one door, and two windows. There was no steeple, but a stovepipe poked skyward through the shingles. It never had a lick of paint on the clapboards or even varnish on the piano. Like the Dreamtime, it also sagged from the secular winds. In central Texas, it was the breakup of communities brought by disastrously low world prices for cotton, and it was the paved highway that carried fathers' sons away from their affection for the earth and to the movie shows in town, where life was different.

I reached part VII of Strehlow's book, on *Love of Native Soil*. My concentration had just begun to slip, my eyes to move away in a direction of their own, when I felt myself awakened by depictions of Aranda men, by the way they stoked my memories of my dad at home in Texas, in Poblado. "Mountains and creeks and springs and water-holes are, to him, not merely interesting or beautiful scenic features in which his eyes may take a passing delight; they are the handiwork of ancestors from which he has descended. The whole countryside is his living, age-old family tree. He will always speak of his 'birthplace' with love and reverence. Today, tears will come into his eyes when he mentions an ancestral home site…"

My father's mortal ancestors did not shape their land out of some primordial ooze. They bought it. Yet, in time, after only a couple of generations, they were committed to it. The connection between my father and his country was a basic one: the springs whose water ran across the limestone bedrock into Poblado Creek and the sinuous live oaks that had been old when he was born, he was a part of them. What I had once dismissed as mere sentiment, I now could see, had been the hub of his existence. Poblado village and its creek remained my father's heart place to his death.

Who would not be moved by the lament of Strehlow's friend Gurra who saw his sacred waterhole dynamited by the white men for their cattle? "And now the soak has almost gone dry. No longer do men pluck up the grass and the weeds and sweep the ground clean around it; no longer do they care for the resting place of Karora. Our young men do no longer care for the traditions of their fathers."

Dad's attachment to his father's "estate" was not the same as the Arandas', but I could see the common root of both. Somehow it had not run through me; in me it stopped, and I was now the poorer man.

I was alone, surrounded by strangers in the middle of Australia, with both my feet on a brass rail, and dropping tears into my beer. I could see that my daddy sent me on this errand to return a fragment of another's lot, to remind me of my own. Either I had stumbled into what his gift had been all about, or else I had drowned my good sense with bereavement and beer. That was quite enough. I needed air, the night's bracing chill.

I swung my satchel off the floor, landing it on the bar with a *thunck* and lifted the flap an inch to peek inside. The stone looked just the same. I gathered my photocopies, left behind some unfamiliar paper money, and pushed through the twin doors out onto the street. There was something about the moon. I steadied myself against a tree to have a look. The slenderest of crescents, light as a pin-feather, it seemed buffeted in a celestial breeze.

10

REGISTRATION for the Rock Art Congress began in the morning, and I arrived early wearing my only pressed shirt. Murray, the conference chair, had written to me that this would be a most important gathering. High-level specialists from all over the world would be present, as well as some South African Bushmen, a delegation of Maoris from New Zealand, the Hopi Tribal chairman, and, essential to my purpose, a significant number of the Aboriginal "traditional owners" of this, their ancestral land. It is to these men in their oxford cloth shirts that I would hand over my father's stone.

What was just as important to me was Murray's assurance that his association was "strongly committed to the Aboriginal control of Aboriginal material culture." This was a noble goal, and one I shared.

"The handing back of your stone," Murray had told me, "would be a symbolic act of practical significance," and whatever he meant by that, I bought into this as well. Furthermore, he intended that my on-stage handover of the stone would be a "celebration of reconciliation."

I had mentally rehearsed his plan. He emailed me, "I would envisage that you give a speech, with the artefact concealed, and the senior custodians for the area then come forward, say some words of gratitude; it will be a kind of goodwill ceremony, one in which you 'bring the stone home.' "

The optimism of his proposal, that "we might start a fashion," overlooked the fact that the repatriation of tjurunga was already an established practice. Australian museums had been doing it for years.

71

And Australian activists had reach: from New York's Natural History Museum to the Vatican. So what I took Murray to mean by "fashion" was that I, having traveled from America with my dad's stone, would be offered as a symbol of *individual* initiative. My hand back, Murray promised, would be "a major media event."

But my segment on the conference program still needed to be scheduled, and the participants corralled. I left a message for Murray at the registration desk, then sat down in the lobby to wait. From my bench I had a view of the conference center's floor-to-ceiling stained glass windows whose luminous red-toned tribal patterns were sharply projected by the morning sun into the vestibule. Dreamtime figures stalked among concentric circles, along pathways arching between them. The early registrants, as they milled about in all the colors, seemed to be composed of myth and made of light, and the world appeared completely changed. I followed a caricature of ants with swollen amber bellies as they stepped off of the glass and onto the floor; they left a trail of incised oval objects terminating at my feet.

"Mark?"

A man was striding toward me with his hand held out. "Mark, I'm Murray." A half dozen years my senior, he was wearing an artfully battered field jacket, a crisp baby-blue shirt, and a well-knotted yellow tie; he looked the part of a gentleman soldier.

"Mark," he said, "we've got a problem." He led me out of the foyer and into the palm grove directly in front where, I supposed, we could talk shielded by the screeching of parrots perched in the fronds above us.

"The Strehlow Research Centre," Murray pointed through the trees to a modern structure fronted by a three-story rammed earth wall, "that's it over there. It's our conference co-sponsor. They're threatening to withdraw support and walk out if we carry through with what you and I have planned. I'm really very sorry, Mark, but we just can't afford it."

"They're threatening to what? But how could . . .?"

"They're the state-sponsored conscience vis a vis disassociated cultural property. We have no choice here, Mark."

Then I understood. The Research Centre was the Jewel House for Theodore Strehlow's "crown jewels," his impounded collection.

Murray continued, "Just let me say that the SRC comprises an important collection of artifacts that Aboriginal men want returned to them, but this has been refused. On the other side of town is the Central Land Council that wants the storehouse thrown open. It's all political, Mark. Highly radioactive politics. We cannot get caught up in all this ill will. I'm sorry." Murray patted my shoulder and left me there.

I paraded once around the grove kicking at loose rocks, looking up occasionally just to glower at the SRC. But my conference entrance fee was taken care of, and I had no other plans. I joined the throng as it moved into the great hall.

For three full days the Rock Art Congress was a camel market of research data and novel theories, with sessions ranging from epistemology to the aesthetic experience of rock art. Australian tribesmen had been maintaining their murals for ten thousand years and *continued* to do so, yet the rushed recital of academic papers seemed beside the point, without a base in life.

Then onto the stage stepped a tiny man, Bill Harney, enlisted to headline a series titled Indigenous Perceptions. "The Dreaming Ancestors," he said, "created a large part of the rock art we see today," and those ancient ones had "put all the laws, ceremonies and stories in place to be handed down."

Harney was a senior Elder of the Wardaman community located in sub-tropical country way up Northern Territory. It was, he said, a land "of tabletop mountains where you can see for miles over the black-soil flood plains, all covered in bush foods and medicine, and with Aboriginal tools lying around all over the place from the old days." He was here to recite his people's Dreamtime story of origins.

"It'll take a while," he cautioned. "But I'll give you the best creation story you've ever had."

It was like the Old Testament stories that I learned in Sunday School but with a wholly different cast of characters. Harney quoted the Rainbow Serpent, " 'I've got to bring the water right across the country. We want everybody underwater.' And ol Rainbow went back and sang a great expressive song and he made the water rise. He brought the water right across the country, flooded up the world."

Behind Harney, making him look even smaller, was projected a huge photograph of a cave painting representing Jabiringa and Yagd-jagbula, the Lightning Brothers, their forms floating side by side with bugged eyes and hair spiked from the electrostatic charge they carried. Harney told their tale, how they restored the land after the flood.

"All these little lightnings jumped off, went across and said, 'We might sing, and stop the water from comin back.' And they put a power on it with a great big song. And that's why the sea is where it is today and can't come back inland any more.' And they talk about, 'that's good and we can go out hunting for food.'

"Now if you're walking around in the muddy land you'll see their footprints in the mud and also in the rock paintings today like this one here behind me."

Afterward, at the break, I edged through the crowd and slipped beside this man. His lovely smile looked straight up at me. I wanted to know if what I had witnessed on my way up from Adelaide was something supernatural. I asked him, "Were the rainbows I saw from my train, dropping from the clouds, in and out of the earth, the body of *the Serpent?*"

"Mighta been him," he said, then dropped down on his heels, tipped back his hat and launched into an impromptu dissertation on the Rainbow Serpent. I squatted down beside him, someone brought paper cups of tea, and in moments we had attracted quite a little crowd. He wrapped up with, "Go an buy me book. Just come out. *Born Under the Paperbark Tree.*"

That afternoon in town I bought his book, and it resolved a confusion I had been having. It turned out that there were two Bill Harneys who were well-known in Australia: the Wardaman tribal Elder, and his white father William E. (Bill) Harney, the bush poet and storyteller of the rugged Outback. Their personal stories were revealed in *Paperbark Tree.*

Bill's father to be, William Harney, had returned from soldiering after WWI, disgusted with the discipline and the waste, fed up with all the killing. He struck out on horseback deep into the still-wild Northern Territory. The stories he told of his adventures there made him a national figure, Australia's best-loved bushman poet and author. Harney, the son, was bush born – "none of that hospital stuff for me" – and had worked, as many Aboriginals had, half time on a cattle station. With the coming of the wet season, those ranch hands walked away "cock-rag and spear" to their river camps and escarpment shelters.

When old Harney died in 1962, schoolboys across Australia were made to memorize one of his poems. I still have my classroom copy of *Australian Poets Speak*. It is full of odes to the great Outback life: men a-shearin sheep, a-drovin cattle; small towns like Oodnadatta, Pepegoona, Arkaroola, Tantanoola; and all the small town politicians, the squatters, and sundowners. Here are poems about lack of rain, the sounds of the bush, and the mateship of men who labored and endured so far from home.

Old Harney worked his way down from the Top End to the Centre. While sitting atop a diesel grader, its wheels "awhirl in a red dust swirl," he pushed through the first road to Ayers Rock, and composed a poem. This was the poem I had chosen to recite before my classmates at Prince Alfred Prep. While sharing with young Harney's Dreamtime story the sensuality and the violence of tooling the earth, this poem sets into ditty a white man's loutish penetration of dark and virgin loam.

> *The honey ants are rooted out to roll upon the sand,*
> *But ever the ramping, stamping fiend goes roaring through the land.*
> *The tyres grind and the steel blade cuts the pads where camels trod*
> *And claws at the ground of a stony mound where tribesmen praised their God.*

And on it goes in trifling rhyme.

The elder Harney writes openly about relations between white Territorians and black women but, his son notes, he never had to answer for the half-caste children he had sired, the ones he left behind.

As a light-skinned half-caste child, young Harney might have been taken away from his indigenous family, through the forces of welfare and "improvement." His mother hid his face behind blackcurrant plum and charcoal, and in September of his twelfth year, "when the flowers came on the coolebah," it was time for him to become a man. Lain across the backs of six grown men, he had his penis ringed with a stone knife. And the stories meant for manhood were brought out, stories illustrated through the spirit paintings found on rock.

Born Under a Paperbark Tree, begins with the words, "My father, old Bill Harney, was a white man." And it was not until just before his death that he invited down his son to see him in the south. Reading to the end, I waited, wanting for Bill to be openly angry about something: the tribal mortifications required to establish manhood, years of squalid conditions in family camps on the cattle stations, the fracture within his family that festered after his sister was abducted by the state, or simply that he never figured in any of his father's books. But the anger never comes. He understands and he accepts. He forgives. And this, for better or for worse, has been his life.

I asked Bill if I might use the creation story he had told if ever I should write this whole thing out and he said yes, that's just fine, and requested only that I recognize his people. It is the Wardaman who generation after generation have kept the story from expiring, keeping it from wearing itself out. It belongs to them, he's just here to tell it, and he's glad I listened.

Between sessions, when tea was set out in the foyer, I would buttonhole one of the speakers, drawing him aside, and ask questions. These were cracker-jack professionals who could have easily cold-shouldered a non-credentialed outsider, or been suspicious of a New Age interloper searching for fairy rings. But they came with me to the palm grove and I showed them the face of my tjurunga – its central spiral and the concentric circles here and there, rippling like raindrops on still water.

I asked these fellows, why the worldwide universality of concentric circles in rock art? "I suppose the more simple the icon, the more likely to be found in different cultures." What of the infinitely more sophisticated spiral? "One might postulate an evolutionarily advanced art stage. It's all very ambiguous." Most importantly, I wondered, do they signify? "The circle? The epitome of exclusion. And, ahh…the supreme spiral: the symbol for inclusion." My last interview concluded with, "Let me know when you find out."

The last that is, until I managed to entice the venerable anthropologist Carol Mancy out to the grove. She was a matronly woman who brooked no foolishness. "Put that thing away," she said, "and let me explain something to you. Your stone configures a complex mythology. It is a diagram of cosmic order. The whole Dreamtime telescopes down into the tjurunga stone. It isn't just a symbol of the Dreamtime, either. It embodies it. It *is* it."

"Look," she said, planting a knee on the ground, and sweeping away the clutter of leaves. "Your stone tells the story of one Dreaming character's adventures. Its story begins inside the Earth. That is its essential potency." She made a spiral in the dirt. "It emerges here, up from, say, a water hole, in human or animal form." She drew a circle alongside the spiral. "It's alive, it's in motion. He makes his camp – that's the first circle. Then his pacing around his fire is marked by the second." She added a third and fourth circle and joined them all with arcing lines. "He's traveling about the countryside shaping the land here, and here, ending up at camp back here." She jabbed her finger into the center of the spiral. "The being goes back down whence he came. It resumes its immaterial form but leaves its tjurunga body topside for the people. It leaves itself to their care. But that's the simple part," she said, rising and dusting off her hands. "Now, look at the principal figure, but not as simple rings laid flat. Think of it as something else – as a portal between the world above and the world below." And Mancy's finger began a sweeping descent toward the ground. "It spirals downward like a staircase. It is the access point between the present and the past, between death and rebirth.

"The Dreamtime potency must be continually drawn up through the portal by ceremonial performance. Every important life form is sustained this way. Aboriginals paint the portal on the ground. You'll see this yourself at the conference closing. It's a ground painting, and it makes the hidden visible. Now you can see it, touch it. Now it's gone." Her foot swept everything away and it was all just like before, simply, only sand.

Mancy was called inside and I was left looking at the earth beneath my feet. Why had I been so sure that this ground, the home of the "traditional owners," would support and not swallow me?

A small fire had been kindled and its smoke gathered in the tree branches so that the dappling light was diffused, and the air sweetened. Six men, white-bearded confreres of the possum totem, stripped to the waist but still topped by cowboy hats, labored silently on their knees. For over an hour they placed pinch by pinch of tufted, ochre-stained plant material onto the ground and, ring by ring, alternately red and white, the mandala grew.

"This has not been witnessed," a man on my left assured me, "by more than a hundred white people in a hundred years."

After the fifth band had been laid down, the painting was complete. The men stood, then assembled cross-legged at the outermost ring. Each lifted up a pair of hardwood boomerangs and began a rhythmic clacking of descending double notes. It was like the beating of a mechanical heart: CLACK-clack, CLACK-clack, CLACK-clack, the beat periodically pausing for a droning chant, then starting up again with a percussive flutter.

From my right, a man whispered into my ear, "They're singing a power into the center. If they mess it up they won't exalt the spirits. And if they succeed," he added, "there will be more successful mating in the possum population."

From behind us a scholar, out from the SRC scriptorium where he labored over Strehlow's camp diaries, joined in. Pointing at the ground painting he said, "That represents a sacred waterhole. A spring. I've been to the site. Still exists on a cattle station. Problem is, the stockmen stuck a pipe right down it. Use it to water their cattle. No problems, though, the Elders say. 'Those blokes won't be here long and the spring'll be flowing after they leave.' Irony is, the possum is extinct around here and has been for fifty years."

He had just confirmed Mancy's suggestion from the day before, that my tjurunga's central icon was a bull's eye centered over an actual site. *My stone was engraved with its own directions to home.* It was readable as an overhead view of the landscape. That's how I put it to him.

"Yeah, your stone's a map," he said. "But then again it's not. The Aboriginals see history written on every surface of their land. We go two kilometers out and it all looks the same, vacant. Now, you say, I'll walk out there and triangulate the icons. But you won't. You can't." What he was telling me was that although my stone's grid of icons did indicate some actual country, it performed only as well as a compass whose needle will not register.

At the furthest edge of conceivability, the stone I carried, loosened but not cut off from its mythological moorings, was following a pre-determined course. It was on its own path. It was very wide, a path onto which my father first, and now I, had meandered. Just out of sight there was a place at which the stone, and whatever restless spirit stirred inside it, wished to end its journey.

Sung over and now become sacred, every scrap of the ground painting's material was carefully collected into buckets and hidden away. The crowd began to part, creating a corridor for a dozen barefoot women shuffling and stomping toward the center, their bare chests painted with the possum icon. Clack, clack went the boomerang chorus. "I've seen better," someone said, a little ungenerously I thought, though I myself was stifling yawns and sweeping little arcs into the dirt with the point of my shoe. I made a slow retreat, edging back toward the fence surrounding Twin Sisters Hill, also known as Kungka Kutjarra Yanga Yanangi Kangkuru. "Sacred Hill," the sign said, "Stay Off."

An old Aboriginal gentleman stood there all alone. I recognized him from the conference's opening ceremony where he had been seated among the traditional owners of Alice Springs: Rupert Maxwell Stuart. Max smiled at me through tobacco-yellowed teeth, those that had not been knocked out in tribal ritual or in prison. His eyes were rheumy, his girth impressive; he was a chain smoker, and of course he wore a western hat. He leaned against the rail watching the dance performance with a proprietary air.

To the folks of Alice Springs, Max is homegrown nobility. Once on trial for his life, he not only escaped the white man's gallows but survived the unintended sentence of many Aboriginal prisoners: "death in custody." After release from his life sentence at Her Majesty's prison at Yatala, and even during a decade of repeated parole violations and re-confinement, Max rediscovered religion – that real old time religion. And he took it to town.

As I sidled up to Max, I knew some of his history from the scuttlebutt exchanged between sessions at the conference. Max was one of Alice Springs's most revered Aranda men, ceremonially and politically. He had helped displaced Aboriginals navigate white law, resulting in half the hereabout land being returned to Aboriginal ownership. And he had initiated into *traditional* Law the man who occupied the highest national office yet held by a native. Max was party to, in the last year of his parole, the negotiations that deeded Ayers Rock, thereafter named Uluru, to its traditional owners. And three months before my arrival in the Centre, he had acted the gracious host to Queen Elizabeth during her second visit to Alice Springs. He would quote Her Majesty from their encounter: "How you going, Max?"

My finding Max under the Twin Sisters Hill was, perhaps, not a coincidence. I waited for him to speak.

With a nod at the huddle of academics in front of us, Max introduced himself, "I never went to school, you know? Wouldn't know, whacha callim, a pencil if I saw one." He continued between pulls on his cigarette, "Maybe one time I was a good Sunday School boy. But I was a donkey." He chuckled. "Now I gotta work to help my people be human, not one a them animals." He took the last hot pull. "Maybe some people say we might be a dying race," he crushed the butt into the dirt, "but I don't think so."

"G'day," I said, my lame attempt at the dialect. "The name's Mark. I'm from the United States. Here to bring back a tjurunga." Max hefted another cigarette from his pack and lit it before turning his head to look at me. He waited for me to say something else.

And I did. I told him about my father. I told him about his time here, about the stone.

"I didn't grow up with my daddy," he said, "else he might've snapped me round a bit if I wasn't doing the right thing, you know. But I can see your daddy musta been a smart fella, puttin you on the right track, hey?"

"Thanks, mate," I said

"Your daddy wanted that tjurunga, like for one a them keepsakes. But inside of him, he's thinkin he shouldn't a take that thing back to America. Maybe it wasn't im thinkin, it was someone else thinkin for im, something whisperin inside his heart, you know?" Max got the *keeping* part exactly right. And the *whispering*, that was the Boy Scout in him, I suppose, the same part of him that wrote in his memoir "the stone should go home."

I said, "I'm doing this for him."

"Them sacred objects got a lot of meaning for us blackfellas. I'm proud of this very good news of that stone coming home. I'll sleep good tonight thinking of that."

After a moment's reflection, he continued, "I think maybe God helped bring em back to us. Like with them Twelve Commandments. Moses went up the hill. He never got a book. We think maybe God gave Moses this rock. He give it to all us – blackfella, whitefella, even purple one." Max offered me a cigarette, which I accepted even though I hadn't smoked in years. He lit another for himself. "I got my piece of that rock at home. My people's stone come back a long way from Germany. No-one come into that room, maybe just me when I want, you know, to think about them things. Dreaming stuff. Just sitting there alone listening...what do you call it...?"

"Meditating?"

"Yeah, meditating. You're thinking, you're learning. More you think, more that thing gonna whisper in your ear. Listen to that slate. Now when the day is done, I'm laying down and the tele is goin. Switch that off. I'm thinkin, good book there. Forget about that book. Laying there. Think. Yeah. There's a lot of meaning to that. The wagon wheel move through the air little bit at a time. That's how life goes, you know? If that wheel don't work, well, we're buggered."

In his pause for a drag I asked, "And you think my helping this tjurunga stone get back into the right hands will…help keep the wagon wheel rolling?" The mob of people in front of us began to break up, stepping aside for the dancers' exit.

"Honestly," I said, "I don't know what I'm doing. How should I, do you think, find who this belongs to?"

"Same like when another tribe has someone else's thing, they're gonna look for the Elders round about, ask em, show em, tribe to tribe to tribe, you know, try to identify it proper way. Then more important, song by song. Where'd you say it come from?"

"Well, Uluru. Supposedly it was stolen from Uluru."

"Anangu there, you know?"

"What's Anangu?"

"The old fellas livin at Uluru. You better go an ask em there. You think you can find that Uluru?"

I knew from the window posters and the sidewalk rate boards on display at every travel agency in Alice Springs that Uluru was somewhere in the vicinity. It was a luminous orange monolith, and it had waited patiently over hundreds of millions of years for tourism's human swarm to find it. That was my stone's destination. Now I was nothing more than its mule, set to move it along its predetermined course. I thought it whispered in my ear and said "Uluru."

I turned to Max to thank him, to bid him farewell, but he was already gone. All that remained was the coiling wisp of smoke he left behind.

11

SITTING STREET SIDE at a restaurant, I had a clear view of the glittering firmament overhead. Earlier, I had phoned Allen, explaining why I was still out here. "Not too badly beat up?" he asked. He was concerned, and this pleased me.

"This stone's goin ome," I had assured him. "Little dingo's caught the scent and the blood's up." I clicked off, then said "Home!" to the pup waiting at my feet.

I poured from a well-chilled bottle of South Australia's Eden Valley wine: "classic apricot and white peach flavours combined with citrus freshness and a hint of spice."

A collection of Uluru brochures was spread out before me. "Learn the real meaning and history of Uluru directly from local Aboriginal Guides. Anangu believe their ancestors have lived at Uluru since the beginning of time." That would cover the epoch in which a white camel-borne explorer had felt free to pilfer their tjurunga. The Anangu must still be mourning my stone's absence. It would be received from me and replaced into some crevice, the keeping place for their sacred objects.

My scheme was perfectly accompanied by the fruity wine. I toasted to its success with a fresh pour. And it was then, over my goblet's rim, that I saw her.

Tall and slender, in a black shift that favored her slight figure, her hair let down for the evening, she walked in among the tables. Younger and prettier than I ever will be again, still she was not exactly beautiful. But she was alluring, and I was not the only man, or woman, to notice this. She stopped, a hand on her hip, looking around for somewhere she could sit.

"Join me," I said, rising from my chair just so.

"I know you," she said, "from the conference. You were talking to Bill Harney." She pulled out the seat opposite mine and slid right in.

"You are one of us?" she asked. "A Rainbow Warrior?"

I had no idea what that was but I did not deny it.

The waiter appeared, gave us menus, and left with our orders.

She said her name was Karla. "I'm from Salzburg." She felt the pull, she said, the shift of energy that moves from Untersberg into Uluru and then back.

"You look at a globe," she said, drawing a circle in the air before me. She pointed, "one is here and the other there. And there should be no connection, but the Serpent is on the move," and she closed her eyes to feel the breeze against her face. Now she appeared not just alluring, but beautiful.

"The Serpent," I said. "Yeah. Bill Harney..."

"You have to open your heart if you're to hear."

"Yes," I said. "You're right."

"And you can only do so through complete surrender."

"Yes," I said. "Surrender."

"Unconditional love."

"Unconditional."

"You have to open yourself."

"You must be open. Yes."

Her collarbone made a shallow bowl that my tongue might easily explore. I poured her the last goblet-full from my bottle.

She said, "The center of all sacred energy forces is right here. Uluru."

"Oh yes," I said and licked a drop off the neck. "I'm going there tomorrow." I told her about the tjurunga. She nodded as though she had known this all along.

She raised her glass to me and laid the rim to her lip. I could trace the wine's chill passing down through her body. "Burrr," she said and threw back her head, shaking out her hair, long and lustrous.

I pointed overhead and said. "Look. There's the Southern Cross." She glanced up.

"No," she rejoined. "You are wrong."

"Karla, I want to kiss you."

"Whatever for?" She was still scanning the sky. "There!" she said, pointing southeast.

"Karla, I want to make love to you."

"Don't be horrible," she spoke into her plate as it was being set down. He set mine down, too. "There is something I want to show you. Eat."

A LL YOU PEOPLE *who live on this land, we gotta stick together, we gotta take a....*

Speeding out of Alice Springs toward Uluru, the reception on the radio was breaking up. I thought about the members of this rock band from the tiny settlement of Santa Elena, young and hungry and searching.

So learn while you can, about your Dreaming...
It was coming in and out.
We've been on this land forever...our spirits on this land.....
Here in this land for....
And it was gone.

My road ran straight and flat through a nearly featureless countryside. FLOODWAY signs were posted but only narrow stands of eucalyptus trees, meandering across the red earth, proved the occasional waters' course. I had the Uluru Road to myself, stopping only once in deference to a feral camel that stepped into my path. Black tire tracks scorched onto the road here at her accustomed crossing. Then I was on my way, eyes fixed on the horizon where the bleached sky merged with asphalt. My mind, though, kept pulling back to Karla and the time we spent together last night, after dinner.

We paid our separate checks and left under dim light, the sparseness of the moon. She was an author, a writer of travel books, and a freelance tour guide. But tonight, she said, she was taking me for a special walk.

She drove us out of town on the Ross Highway. A couple of miles past the last light she pulled off the road, stopping moments later at a chain barrier. She switched off her motor and headlamps. The dark and silence rushed up around us, just as the waters swallow a ship at sea. I followed her out of the car.

Our path wound between huge, heaped boulders, their shadows so utterly empty and bottomless that out of caution I sidestepped around them. Karla glided over it all, her hand stroking the air. She whispered, "Do you feel that?"

And walking a little further, she stopped. "It's a spirit line." Then pivoting to the right, "The power is stronger here."

I was treading along, close on her heels, watching my feet.

She said, "You feel it here, don't you?" I came ahead into the dark, and we collided.

"Karla, I'm no good at this. I'm a photographer. I need to see what I'm looking at for this to work." I had spent a few weeks in a desert before, in West Texas, during high school, making pictures in the low, raking light. Every rock, dry creek bed, bluff and sand grain was akin, each to the other. Every square foot of it was an articulation of the larger composition. It was comprehensible, like a diagram of something animate at work.

I had those feelings then, and I posted letters home to Dad during those weeks. I wanted him to know that I saw the logic in geophysics, and then some. I once felt, while standing on a bluff in a quiet evening, that something new, something vital in me, was coming to be, that this material landscape was being transformed into something more. My mistake, of course, was telling Dad that I was "getting messages."

"Mystics met their god in the desert once upon a time," he wrote me back. "Boys alone at night *hear things*." I never wrote to him again.

"I get it," I said to Karla. "You feel a flow of energy. You feel its presence. Back in the desert I thought I sensed something, too. But I lost it, whatever it was. Can you understand?"

Karla was silent. I was sorry to disappoint her. I asked her about the Rainbow Serpent, her affinity, and she answered slowly, as if reluctant to be drawn into words.

"I did go to Utopia. A miserable place. I was approached by this man who told me, 'You are a snake Dreaming. Do you know this?' 'Yes,' I said to him, 'That is what I am.' He asked me to go with him out into the bush, to be initiated. I said, 'No.' "

"Karla, how could an Aboriginal man initiate *you*, a woman, into anything?"

"He wanted to place a crystal in my forehead, here." She lifted my finger to her hairline.

"You mean, to lay it on your skin."

"No, place it into my forehead and one behind each ear. This would give me the clear vision."

"I can see why you declined."

"It was a test. They are always testing you, these ones, just as they are testing their young men. They want to see if you are sincere in your belief, if you have what it takes to reach a further level on the way – reach for the truth.

"But that night he sent to me a dream. I was the Rainbow Serpent. It was sensuous, and very beautiful. My body was made of crystal. The rainbow colors circled me and I journeyed through the earth. There were no obstacles and I did pass with ease."

She turned away and looked behind her toward a sloping rock face. She placed herself atop it – perhaps, I thought, to lay herself down for me. But she draped one arm over the other, sitting upright. The crescent moon was suspended above her, sharp-pointed like a scimitar. It rimmed her in its silver light. I blinked.

She asked, "What about *your* journey? Where is it taking *you?*"

I felt the sand shift below my feet. "I thought this trip would bring me closer to my father."

"You are your own person. Do you think that your father's life is yours? Are there not things that you can know, which he never could?

"Yes, you're right."

"Then what is it you want here, with his *sacred* stone?"

"Theodore Strehlow wrote that..."

"Have care," she interrupted, "with Strehlow and other 'Aboriginal Studies' people. They cannot explain the spiritual, mental and psychic knowledge of old cultures. You cannot do this as an observer, at a distance. Tell me, what is it you are afraid of?"

"Afraid?"

"Yes. I think for you that 'scared' and 'sacred' mean the same. You are scared of me right now."

"Maybe a little."

"So you would make love to me. Why is that? You wish to slay me? To dispel your fear?"

I had no reply.

"Mark, where is your *heart?*"

She said, "It is okay. We go now."

On the road back to Alice Springs a violent side wind buffeted Karla's little SUV and carried in a faint aroma of smoke. Far off in the distance, a brush fire sparkled along the horizon, looking like a procession of torchbearers. She gripped the wheel tightly, struggling to stay on course. "You see strange things out here at this hour," she said. "Once an Aboriginal man crossed my lights. Dressed only in ceremonial paint. He walked off into the night. Anyone who works out here sees these things."

She pulled up to the curb, in front of my hostel. I felt bruised and hollowed out. I whispered, "Thank you," and pushed open my door. One foot on the curb, I was stopped by Karla's hand. I slid back into my seat. "Mark," she said, "you are not horrible. I am sorry I said this to you. It is okay. You may kiss me." She leaned forward to offer her cheek, which I kissed lightly, dryly. "You are a good person, Mark, but you are a boy. This is a big journey you are on. There are things here that your camera cannot tell you. You can only see these things when you are ready to step into this other dimension of life. This can only happen through your heart. That's the doorway." She peered at me over her glasses. I was closing the door when she called, "Wait." She reached to the floor. "Here. You will want your stone."

The Report of the Horn Scientific Expedition describes it thus: "Above the yellow sand and dull green Mulga rose the Rock – a huge dome-shaped monolith, brilliant Venetian red in colour. A mile in length, with its sides rising precipitously to a height of eleven hundred feet above the plain, it stands out in lonely grandeur against the clear sky."

Karla saw Uluru through a different lens, as the "center of all sacred energy forces." Uluru, then, was a natural temple. Karla, who I had come at like a randy teenager, wanted me to get this right.

Nearing the Park boundary, I was thinking about the things Karla said, and about my grandfather's faith, and what might be possible for me to know here. What was it really that I wanted with my stone? Without thinking much further, I just knew, and if I am honest with myself I always did, that what I wanted more than anything was to experience – to feel as strongly as Karla did, with the conviction of my grandfather's devotion to his earth – the *sacred*. I did not, do not, think of myself as religious. But if I were to witness, or better, to somehow share with the Anangu the tjurunga's primal power, then I might know. I shuddered at the prospect.

The Luritja Road cut in from the north bringing traffic down from Kings Canyon, and there were the inevitable tour busses. I merged into a chain of cars and campers, slithering over sand hills, mounting modest rises, gently dropping down the basins, with curves just round enough to hide the road's end. I watched ahead for the unexpected.

A pungent scent from nearing rain blew through my car windows, messenger from a bank of dark clouds sweeping over the western horizon.

As the storm darkened Uluru came into view a raindrop hit my windshield, pitting its film of sand. At first, it was a few stray drops, then heavier and in very little time it was a deluge. But as I pulled into the National Park's first Viewing Area, it was already over, and wispy vapors were lifting off Uluru's violet-blue surface. At my feet rivulets of water coursed between clumps of spinifex grass and yellow-blossomed gravelia, to pool in the damp, deep-hued sand.

The surface of Uluru, which in photographs appears to have no more texture than a loaf of bread, now revealed its deeply carved ravines, each highlighted by foaming water cascading down nearly vertical walls.

For a brief few minutes, until the sheer surface drained off, tributaries fed streams that poured hundreds of feet from spill-offs in wide, furious falls. Elsewhere, a rivulet descended languorously through a stair-stepped series of scalloped stone, a necklace of pools threaded by the white cord of water.

I stood leaning against the rail fence, transfixed as Uluru flashed magenta when spears of sunlight slipped through breaking clouds and jabbed the surface. A faint rainbow evanesced, shimmering against the dull sky. Good day for the Serpent, I thought. She was charged up now.

Backtracking away from the spectacle, I found the campground and paid my way in. Boy Scouts in red kerchiefs were pulling a plastic rain sheet off their fire-pit. I drove past them to find a spot for myself at a distant edge.

13

NYLON RUFFLING in a light breeze, fluttering over my face, dew dripping into the tent. It was dark, well before dawn, and cold. I jumped out of my sleeping bag into the car and revved it up. My headlights swept over trailers and tents as I left, driving for the Sunrise Viewing area at Uluru's eastern face.

The monolith, even up close, was only a hulking black void imposed on a sky brilliantly strewn with stars. The moon, no longer the slender crescent I had seen before, now was swelling, putting on a little belly. Definitely pregnant. I paced up and down the pavement listening to the silence, aware that today was the day I had come to Australia for. As the moon backed away from the brightening eastern horizon, Uluru emerged out of the gloom. For every handful of stars that winked out, a few more cars arrived. Tour buses rumbled in, hissed to a stop, their passengers spilling out and laughing, talking, huddling in the cold. Staccato camera flashes peppered the dawn.

The sun rose. Uluru flushed crimson. The color matured, then within moments it drained away taking along with it all of the enchantment. What remained was merely gigantic, rather forlorn, just a stone. The people boarded their vehicles and sped away for breakfast.

Birds rushed in to fill the renewed silence, flying to the water pools beneath the warming rock face. Wood-swallows, appearing as small as gnats, darted at insects along the cliffs. I got into my car and swung around heading for the Culture Centre.

The parking lot was empty. I entered the building by its cave-mouth door and descended into a dim corridor. On the floor lay a yellow serpent mosaic to guide me along its curves toward Uluru's mythic center. The familiar sounds of ritual surrounded me, the rhythmic beating of sticks, click, clack, click, clack and the chanting of high-pitched voices. Native women flickered onto a wall, their bodies painted over with tribal designs, engaging in a shuffle dance step. The film looped around again and again until I moved on.

At the reception desk a young, uniformed park ranger stood listening into the crackle of a radio transmission. He raised his face and smiled, ready to answer any of the usual questions, to make my visit to Uluru as safe and pleasant as he could. His badge read "Dan." He said, "Yes, sir. How can I be of help?"

I stepped up to the desk and opened my satchel. I brought out the tjurunga and placed it on the counter right between us. I said, "I have come to return this sacred stone."

And without even a glance, he said, "Very well, then, sir. Please serve yourself. There's a place for your stone just over there." He leaned forward and pointed past a video monitor playing a demonstration of the Anangu way to gut a kangaroo, and through a glass door into the yard. "You can reach it right through there."

"We'd be happy to have your comments as well, amongst the others in our visitor book. It's just over there." He pointed behind me to a black ring-binder that lay open on a pedestal. He stood smiling at me vacantly as he refocused on his radio.

I walked over to the glass door and looked outside onto a small pile of stones, natural fragments, bits and pieces of the same gray color as the monolith outside. Ranger Dan's eyes followed me as I moved across the room and toward the binder open mid-volume to a letter date-stamped by the HQ office.

> Dear Sir/Madam Head Ranger:
>
> Enclosed herewith is a rock I brought home from Uluru in 1988. I don't want to go into great detail regarding the suffering this object has brought me, but let me say that the last twelve years have been a long list of unfortunate happenings. One bloody misery

after another. Everywhere this rock has been, misery and grief have followed.

Furthermore, I took photographs of Sacred Sites around the Rock, after being asked not to.

Not a single photograph taken after the incident was any good: out of focus, blurred. Fortunately someone stole the camera.

Kind Regards, [signed],
Gold Coast, Queensland

"Dan," I said, returning to the counter.

"Yes, sir."

"You don't understand."

"No, sir?"

"No. This is a sacred stone – a *real* sacred stone." I lifted up the tjurunga to eye level. His eyes flickered toward the stone and returned to meet mine. "May I speak frankly?" I asked, lowering my voice. "It's a *tjurunga* stone." And plunging ahead, "It's been in my family for thirty years and we think it may have come from Uluru. I want, and maybe you could help me here, Dan, to speak to the Anangu so I can verify what my father was told and return it home."

At the pay phone outside I punched in the number Dan had written out. Archie Saunders, the chair of Mutitjulu Community, answered. "You'd better come around to my office. We're just going into a meeting now and we'll be locked up all day."

There is a photograph my father took of Uluru in 1963, with his Leica, from inside a company plane at about three thousand feet. The flatness that surrounds Uluru is relieved only by undulating sand hills, like a chorus line of snakes, stretching away beyond sight. Down there somewhere Old Bill Harney is grading his road through them, his diesel monster clawing the ground "where the tribesmen praised their God." Barely visible in Dad's photo are four small metal buildings clustered together. Now, decades later, millions of tourist dollars flow into the National Park every year and a portion of this endows the community of Mutitjulu. I found its gravel driveway posted with half a dozen signs, each a different version of "Keep Out."

Waiting for me outside of an adobe, tin-roofed building, his ample belly cinched with a snakeskin belt, and his pleasant demeanor immediately evident, Archie introduced himself. Some years past, Archie had come to the neighboring resort complex as a maintenance engineer for its desalination plant, and then stayed. He became recognized as one of the "traditional owners" of Uluru, and eventually was elected Chairman by Mutijulu's two hundred-fifty Aboriginal residents.

It was in Archie's capacity as liaison for Anangu "cultural protection" that he received me. We sat in his office with the door open. I told him my father's story, so well rehearsed by now that it came out as a litany. Archie, rhythmically tapping a finger on his desk, merely listened to my recital.

"I don't know if you or the Elders in the community have any interest in these objects," I said.

"We do, actually. A couple of years ago I had to go down to the Adelaide museum because someone had sent them a sacred object. It was from here. Mulga Seed Dreaming. I had to bring it back."

"You brought it back to..." and instantly I hoped.

"The Rock, of course. We blocked off part of the road so that the men could do their stuff."

I imagined my own stone placed back on its rightful hearth, its sacredness rekindled. The sacred would flicker. It would manifest in me, as real for me as for the Anangu.

"Would you like to look at it?" I said while gesturing down toward my satchel.

I lay it on his desk and he leaned forward over it, not touching it.

"Hmmm. Hmmm," Archie said. "There's one stone in the cave that'd be so big..." and stretched his hands hip-width, "and it's got this mark right in the center." He pointed down toward the spiral at the center of my stone. "Some stones may have only one mark or only a few, and sometimes more. This stone might be another portion, maybe a piece of the jig-saw puzzle."

"That would be nice."

"I'd like to show it to the old men," he said, "If that's alright. I'm pretty sure they'll pick it out right away. I think they'd know exactly what it means."

"Righty-o, Arch. We're going in now," came a voice from just outside the office, someone on his staff. Archie tossed a newspaper over the stone. A head stuck through the doorway. "You coming, mate? The lawyers're here."

"Yeah, yeah, no worries," Archie said. "I'll be right in." The staffer left.

"So alright then, Mark. Can you come by tonight and I'll let you know what happens? Stop in at our barbie." I assured him that would be just fine; only I had one request.

"If the men do accept the stone and take it into their cave, I want to accompany them. I need to be there."

"Well, I don't know, Mark. I'm not sure how the men might feel about that. Is this your *condition* for its return?"

"No, no, no. Absolutely not," I said, backpedaling as fast as I could. "If the stone's good, it stays. Period. But I need to see…" and I lied, "I'd like to write a story. There are others who'll want to know how the old men brought the stone home. A magazine story, you know?"

"There'd be some problems there, mate." Archie stood and slid the tjurunga, wrapped in newsprint, inside his briefcase. "Look, I've got to be in the meeting, but," he handed me a Visitors Guide, "I'll tell the men what you said and then we'll know."

14

IT WAS a fair day. High, feathery clouds were all that was left of yesterday's storm. There were eight hours remaining before I saw Archie again, eight hours for me to play. I opened the pamphlet he gave me and scanned its roster of tours and times. The morning's first Mala Walk along Uluru's far side had already begun. I set out, determined to be early for the next.

As I approached Uluru's western edge, the park's second most noted sight came into view: the column of hikers trudging in unbroken single file up a thousand feet of bare rock face and down again along the same chain rail. Silhouetted against the sky, they did resemble ants on the march and so *mingas,* the Aboriginal name for tourists, I thought, was apt.

In the parking lot a dozen folks stood waiting in a loose fold with their guide; a private group, I was told. The guide's name was Greta. Whenever the Anangu ranger arrived, she said, the tour would start. I could freeload if I stayed in the back, out of her way.

The ranger, a young Aboriginal man, arrived neatly suited up in pressed khakis and shoulder patches. Greta twisted her long hair up into a coil, knotted it, and then briskly headed down the gravel path with the group at her heels.

They chattered among themselves in German, a language I did not understand, although I heard one couple speaking English. This woman wore a fringed red leather jacket, gaudy glass beads across her shoulders spelling out "TEXAS." In spike-heeled boots, she had the uncertain gait of a child stepping along the top of a fence. Greta and her tourists, with the ranger at a casual distance, arrived at the first Point of Interest.

She led us into a broad shelter that had been carved deep into a rock wall by wind-borne sand. Its rear wall swept high overhead, its crusty lip thrown outward toward the sun, enfolding us in the coolness of its shadow. Projecting from the rear wall was a naturally sculpted bas-relief, somewhat resembling Rodin's *Burghers of Calais* – stricken figures, their faces turned away. Greta had brought us down into Uluru's mythological strata. She knelt down on the sand floor. With the palm of one hand she swept flat a patch before her. We gathered in a circle, the children kneeling in front for a good story.

She drew a diagram in the sand: one circle that she called Uluru, and several more around it as far as she could reach. The figures of Aboriginal mythology, the ones who had visited Uluru, came from – shown by a sweep of her hand – the country all around.

From an outlying ring she dragged two fingers in a serpentine track toward the center. A child called out, "Cobra." Greta nodded. She added dots inside the python's body. "Here are its eggs," she indicated with a hand over her womb. She pointed outside to where the snake had left her eggs behind in the form of two stone marbles.

The outermost circle concerned, as far as I could make out, a pursuit of two women all across the continent by a fellow who would not accept "no" for an answer. This particularly pleased the men in the group, but their wives had the last laugh. The episode concluded at Uluru where the fellow was finally fended off. Greta led us outside to a cleaved boulder, the split head of the pursuer.

The group had walked right over Greta's story in the sand. But before it was completely gone, I knelt and drew around it an ellipse, encircling Uluru, then placed a dot along the line. This would be my stone, in orbit around Uluru's gravitational pull.

Greta, with her tourists clumped behind, resumed the trail leading to the Kantju Gorge, Ranger Michael attending from the rear. I joined him there to see what he had to say.

"These water holes, you know," Michael said to me, gesturing ahead to the Kantju pool. "They're visited by kangaroo. Suppose that's my dinner. Four or five might come to drink and I'll stay back, just watch, let the first one drink. Second one come, third and fourth drink and leave. Now the fifth one has his fill. I let him have his water. But this one he doesn't leave. He gets speared. See, if I jumped the whole mob at once I'd get one or two but the others would run off to another country. Wouldn't come back."

"The fifth kangaroo," I said.

"A hunter has to be that smart, to make sure there's more for later."

A tourist, the man who spoke English, split off and headed right for us. Once, as he and I passed under a bower of trees, this guy had muttered sideways toward me, "If any of those Anangu know anything about this Rock's lore, they learned it from books." He considered himself well-read, and he had questions.

"Yes, of course," the tourist said. "I am a hunter, too. But what about the religion? The ceremonial life?"

Michael's position was one that divided his loyalties. On one hand, this young ranger was a prince, the heir-apparent of a key Uluru Dreaming. On the other hand, he acted the gracious host with a practiced forbearance, revealing only enough to satisfy the tourists.

"My mother's cousin's brother-in-law was the last senior Marsupial Mole man," Michael said. "He died recently. We closed down the Rock."

"I read about that," I piped in. The article had quoted some very disappointed tourists.

"I've been brought up to take his position. My teachers are the old men," he said, lifting his cap and sweeping back his hair. "Because they're senior men, my professors, they wear red hair strings across their foreheads. Yes, that's . . . It's like a university. You know, you wouldn't just decide to become a court judge and suddenly you're a judge."

"And your memory for songs and stories, then?" the tourist said. "You any good?"

"Pretty good. Not every boy goes all the way like in the western schools. Not everybody gets the high degree."

Below the Kantju Gorge, the group had assembled at its brimming waterhole, the end of the trail. When they started for their bus I hung back with Michael. Surely he would know about the older men's connections to tjurunga. I told him all about my struggles with my father's stone. He was interested. This was a story he had not encountered from a tourist before.

"I've got the afternoon off," he said, "I'm driving out to visit my grandfather at Kata Tjuta. If you're free, you could come along. We could talk more then. It will be good for you to know more."

Unlike the monolithic Uluru, Kata Tjuta, some kilometers away, is a cluster of gigantic stone domes. Seeing them at sunset from a distance, the American diarist Elizabeth Dean describes them as glowing "claret red and gold from a purple foundation, looking like a gigantic heap of sapphires, rubies and opals on a russet velvet hand." At mid-afternoon, up close where I was, they were dun-colored camels kneeling heads down, huddled together waiting out a sandstorm. Squeezed between their humps were dry creek beds littered with boulders, and among these grew magnificent white ghost gum trees.

The sun was searing, and before we descended into the first vale even my socks were soaked. "Your grandfather works here?"

"Lives here. On the other side. We'll just have a walk."

I had trouble keeping up with Michael who fairly trotted along the trail. My arms were pin-wheeling outward to keep balance on the steep-sided path. I shouted ahead, "Michael, who are your people? Your family." He slowed.

"My mother's southern Aranda. She never knew her father, an Irishman, a shoemaker she heard, in Alice Springs. She and her mum and step-dad lived off the land, slept under the stars in the creek." He reached for his wallet and fished out a black and white snapshot. "That's her," he said, "my grandmother. Little one's my mum." The picture was of an Aboriginal woman standing chest deep in a hole, resting from a sweat-drenched effort. She is looking at her baby who lays across a heap of earth pulled from the pit. Within reach of the woman are two oblong wooden bowls. One of these was being used to scoop out dirt loosened by her digging stick. The other bowl holds a double-handful mound of glistening orbs, each about the size of a marble. "Honey ants," said Michael. "We was stronger then. No sugar in sacks.

"My mum was seven years old when the Sacred Heart nuns learned about her, this half-caste girl, no lawful father, and went looking for her. She got taken away." He turned to me. "Taken away," he said, "like Stolen Generation. Years later she came back to Alice Springs, still speaking the language, talking Aranda." Then studying the ground at his feet, "Went door knocking for her mum, door to door looking for her. Brave woman."

We walked on some more, and after a bit he said, "I started hanging around with my uncle, going out into the bush, got more interested in going through the men's business. Maybe I'm ready now to learn to be a man. I would've been sixteen. Then me and my younger brother went through the Law together."

"What's *that* like?"

Michael didn't answer. But as we reached the bottom, stopping at a tap to fill my Nalgene, he said, "The red ochre men, you know, the men with the red hair strings, I traveled with them for three months, in the Western Desert – up to Yeundumu, Kintore, and Papunya. In the old days, I'd have walked the story lines and learned them and the songs, as we went along. Now we go out in trucks.

"We'd just drive in. There'd be two old men waiting, one on this side, one on that side, holding up spears like it's a gateway. You gotta run through it and there's some laying into as well. A little break then, a cup of tea and we start the ceremony straight away. We learn about their country, learn where everything is. You learn your boundary lines, where you can go, what you can do. You get to know about this country like a big map, all the invisible paths goin round. And that's what it is. It's about sharing knowledge with the other men. Are you ready?"

We wound our way through the ravine's jumble of boulders, the atmosphere dense with reflected orange light. I stopped once to run my hand across the smooth, chalky skin of a ghost gum. Perched high above was a ringneck, brilliantly colored as an Amazonian parrot. It lifted off with a whistle and flew to another, distant tree.

Still hot, we found some shade. Michael stood before me as I slumped against the cliff wall, wiped my brow, and bent to empty out a pebble from my shoe. He chewed a piece of grass and surveyed the wedge of sky ahead.

I said, "Archie told me that the Elders got a tjurunga back a couple of years ago. When it came up from Adelaide, how exactly did you bring it back to your people, to Uluru?"

"We passed it around. We rubbed it. Rubbed it, passed it around. The men get a bit more strong. We pass it around again. We sang a few songs about it then put it away, back where it belongs. There's a couple of old men come from other communities, come for that special time. That tjurunga was part of their stories, too. We've got a little cave, only that high."

I retied my lace and followed Michael back into the sun, noticeably softened by a few degrees. While we rested, the afternoon had turned a corner toward evening.

"A lot of the old people say that's it, that's the main one – tjurunga, you know – that started everything, the ceremonies. Proper lot. Without em, you wouldn't have the Law. But if you got that there, you hold on to it, you got the Law with you. You can keep the Law strong. That's what the old people still tell us."

We diverged from the creek bed and Michael walked steadily onward. Our new path skirted a wall, steepening as we climbed toward the high, terminal cleft between the canyon's two sides. I found him, and joined him, silently fixed on the panorama ahead of us and far below.

The canyon walls framed our vista, seemed to be funneling and concentrating its effect. Rising out of a broad valley whose contours were draped in swaths of sage forest, were dozens of orange domes – like Buddhist stupas, I thought – some small, others mounting over the horizon. The yellow-tinged light of the lowering sun caressed everything in the valley like a blessing. The land was alive. It was sensitive as a lover's body, almost swelling with breath, rippling with – I had no better words for this – spiritual energy. I felt quite dizzy and had to sit down on a rock. Michael smiled.

"Your grandfather lives out there?" I sputtered.

"No, you'll see. It's around this side."

"He's an *it*? Not a *he*? Michael, are you taking me to visit your tjurunga?"

"No, I'm not. You'd have to pay for that, pay what I paid."

"And how much would that be?" as though I could barter.

"What I've already said, what I told you. A good hiding. Right-o, Mark. Got your balance? You're going to need it."

We did not continue on the trail, which descended into the valley. We cut left, skirting around the face of the mountain in a slow, rising spiral, one hand touching rock and the other only air.

We arrived at a ledge, a bench cut deeply into the nearly vertical face. Michael stopped as though a door stood before us. He knelt down and brushed aside the yellow grasses that spiked the air; he sipped some of yesterday's rainwater where it collected in a small basin. Over his back I studied a copse of gnarled evergreens that had rooted themselves in the ledge fissures.

These trees had shed scraps of themselves to make a bed of bark and twigs and needles around their trunks. Where long ago a whole branch had dropped off, it lay unmolested, hanging over the ledge, yielding its rigidity to time and molding itself to the rock.

How tempting it would be to believe that this all had been here forever, how easy to assign to the old tree a spirit as ancient as the day of creation. The tree was vital even as smaller deaths lay all around. I saw endurance without pomposity, and a serenity that seemed to be drawn from all the elements.

Michael offered no formal introduction but silently brought me into his grandfather's company. We sat with our backs to the ledge and gazed past the old tree's trunk, twisted into sandy humus like a corkscrew. We watched what it watched. Out of silence came the gentle entanglement of air in the needles, a voice without words. I felt, rather than noted, the earth's rotation.

"Grandfather here, he's a good teacher," Michael said, stirring.

"Hmm," I said.

"There's a lot of teachers in my class family. They're my grandfathers, too. Well-respected Law men, they are. A lot of stories, a lot of songs there." Michael stepped away, careful not to crush a single twig, and jerked his thumb back at his tree. "Other main teacher is this one here."

We retraced our path back to the car, and this time it was easier, somehow it seemed shorter. The chirps and hums and trills of nocturnal creatures rose out of Kata Tjuta's dark ravines. Looking up now and again, I glimpsed distant Uluru, the late sun searing its summit red, and lower down, its slopes a somber shade of umber.

Michael radioed Mutitjulu from his car, and someone went looking for Archie. "Ask him," I urged.

Archie had not had time to draw the old men aside, but he would do so right away, he told Michael. He wanted us to join them for the barbecue. He referred to it as "the event," and it would be held at the Culture Centre.

Michael spoke, "I'll drop him off directly," and signed out. Michael wanted to go home to Mutitjulu, to be with his family.

My little Ford was there in the Centre's lot, now dwarfed inside a fleet of the lawyers' hulking white Land Rovers. I pressed some money into Michael's hand, unsure if he would want it or how he might feel about the exchange. But I was grateful for the experience, happy to know the man. "This is for the kids," I said. If I saw him again, it would be tomorrow, in his formal role as the junior Marsupial Mole man. He would preside with the Elders, standing at the cave mouth with my tjurunga. I hoped it would be Michael who carried it inside, chants echoing, the awe, the reverence, Michael who would bring the stone home.

15

THE GROVE of desert oak outside the Center had been readied for a party. There was a banquet table set for fifty, and bottles of wine opened at every other place. Paper globes strung between the trees were lit, and a fully costumed grill chef was laying fat steaks across six feet of hot coals. The event had begun, yet I seemed to be the only one who had arrived. Suddenly I was ravenous and moved immediately to get my steak. This was when the bus pulled up and let off its load of Japanese tourists. The steaks were for them. My party, as the chef politely told me, could be found out back. He gestured with his fork, "Over there. It's on the other side."

I walked around the building breathing thick gray smoke, cringing at the smell of burning hair and flesh. Women and children were huddled together around a fire pit into which the un-skinned body of a kangaroo had just been dumped. The men of Mutitjulu were milling about, smoking cigarettes and drinking soda. Two of them wore red headbands, the rest wore cowboy hats. Further on was the contingent of Sydney lawyers, crowded around a gas grill. Their beef patties were being watched, discussed, flipped, judiciously examined and flipped once again.

I saw Archie, the fatigued host, now sporting a Hawaiian shirt. I caught his eye, and he walked toward me. "Mark, how's it going? Come with me?"

He walked me to his car where he removed a parcel wrapped in newspaper from under his seat. He pushed it at me and twined his arms across his chest.

I didn't know what to say.

"Sorry, mate. It's not right."

"I don't understand. How is it not right?"

"I told the old men what you said about your dad and all. They became quite excited. And I told them about your condition for its return…"

"It wasn't a *condition*, Archie."

"…you wanting to be there for its return to the cave. Well, they didn't much like that. You're not the first one, you see, who's come here looking around into their business. It's over the top, mate." Archie looked toward the party and back at me. "But I showed them the stone, like I said. They were quite interested, spent good time with it. But in the end, they decided that it wasn't theirs. Doesn't belong here."

"But how do they know? Maybe they're wrong. Maybe they missed something."

He shrugged his shoulders. "It's in the designs, mate. Mind you, there was some recognition. But these blokes'd know if it was from one of their Dreamings. The Elders got the stories and their designs up here." He tapped his temple. "God gave the Aboriginals their memory and what he gave to you whitefellas…"

"Yeah, I can guess. Floppy disks. But, if it didn't come from here…I mean, what am I supposed to do? How will I know?"

"Craig, our culture-bloke, thought it might've come from further north of here. You could try up that way, see what you can learn. Maybe someone up there will take it back."

Archie offered me a little something as a consolation. "Here, Mark. You've had a big day. Come get yourself a sandwich."

Hungry as I was I couldn't think of eating. I was too upset. But the tjurunga didn't belong here. I had to accept that.

My problem went much deeper. It was with myself that I felt wrong. By asking to be included in the men's affairs, I had polluted my offering and failed the Mutitjulu Elders' righteous scrutiny. I had presumed upon a secret/sacred practice. I felt awful, debased somehow. The image of a despoiler crept into my mind. Allen would be appalled.

How could I have hoped to gain anything from whatever happened inside the folds of Uluru? It was an adolescent's luxuriant desire, a promiscuous pursuit. Like wanting to fuck Karla.

What would I say to her, she who had counseled me to "walk with an open heart" and to make my offering without expecting anything? "If your stone belongs there," she said, "then the loving energy of Uluru, and your own spirit, will have been blessed."

Now everything seemed in doubt. This gravitation of the stone to native landscape, had I made it up? Was "traditional ownership" of Uluru nothing but a fraud? Was *any* of this real? Was I caught up in someone else's hallucination or my own? I wasn't sure that words could sort it out.

I looked down at the tjurunga's imperturbable little Buddha face, thinking, "You led us here, stone. What now? Shall we give *chance* a try?"

I lifted it up onto my car's roof and gave it a spin. The oddly balanced shape turned slowly, wobbled once and stopped, as confounded as I was. So it was now my turn to decide. I put the Pinto into gear.

At the Sunset Viewing Area picnic coolers were being packed away, and lawn chairs handed down from rooftop platforms.

The deep calm that accompanies evening had settled over the land. First stars pricked the sky.

I continued to look back at the darkened Uluru. For a while, it seemed almost to keep pace, a shadow scuttling through the scrub.

16

I REACHED the Ntaria Community Council at Hermannsburg by phone, and they offered me a ride into the village with their driver Robbie. On the truck's gritty metal floor behind us, curled asleep against the mailbag, was a handsome young Aboriginal man just released from police lockup and on his way back home.

Our roadway took the same route as the old camel path between Alice Springs and the Lutheran mission. I held in mind a sentence from a hundred-year-old letter I came across in the Jubilee Reading Room. Richard Threlwall Maurice, dispatched by a financial backer in Adelaide, spent four weeks en route to Hermannsburg from Alice Springs acquiring ethnological specimens. Maurice was the crystallized form of the avaricious, unrepentant collector of tjurunga, so much so that his accumulated burden of tjurunga stones became a hindrance. He wrote to his sponsor from Hermannsburg that the "camels won't stand the stones at present & I know they will have a struggle with the weight they will carry away from here." Had Maurice been forced to abandon one of his camel saddlebags at the mission? Was it from one of his that Dad selected a "pilfered" stone? It was impossible to say. Had my father been told the truth? Was his tjurunga merely acquired, or had it been pilfered? And from this distant point in time, did it even make a difference? I had to remind myself, someone near here was missing his grandfather's tjurunga.

We flashed past the large green sign "National Park" pointing to the right, toward the scenic canyons worn through the MacDonnell Ranges by the headwaters of the Finke River. Theodore Strehlow's account of his childhood in Hermannsburg lay open on my knee, the pages held down against the hot air streaming through the window. He describes this desert in flood, its ancient slumber disturbed by occasional violent dreams: "the two source streams of the Finke River, on whose banks Hermannsburg was standing, rushed down in foaming fury during flood times; and once they had passed the station buildings, these swirling floodwaters penetrated into the broad southern range and dashed themselves…"

The van bumped off the pavement at the turn to Hermannsburg and spit gravel sideways. Alex, the Aboriginal who had been sleeping in the back, woke and pulled himself up to look outside.

Two miles on, we stopped before an iron fence. The plume of road dust that had trailed our van rolled over us in a silent orange fog. Through its thinning edge the old mission materialized. Low stone buildings, plastered brilliant white, improbable as icebergs, sat around a barren yard. One by one, I recognized the buildings from my father's photographs, when the mission had been active. There stood the little schoolhouse, there stood the tannery, a meat house and a bake house, the mortuary, and in the compound's very center, there was the small stone chapel. The bronze bell was the only thing that had changed. In Dad's photo it swung from a rod notched into two magnificent gum trees. Now only one of the trees remained, and the bell and rod listed sideways onto an iron crutch. The entire compound seemed deserted, even by its ghosts.

Among the missionaries once posted here, one name is prominent: Carl Strehlow, Theodore's father. The Strehlow House backed up to a bluff over the temperamental Finke River, its corrugated roof low and broad. Inside, Robbie told me, I would find the Tea Room where the proprietor might get me going. Confirming our return to Alice Springs after the weekend, we shook hands. I pulled my rent-a-tent from his truck and walked across the yard. After passing by the gate and through the rose garden, I dumped my stuff inside the flagstone vestibule. From the cool and dark interior, the air was thick with something sweet, pungent with the scent of cinnamon, buttery moist. I pursued the scent down the corridor.

On a small table was a guest register opened to a nearly empty page. "Tea is at ten," came a woman's voice from down the hall. "But do sign in."

"I'll just look for an entry made by my father," I called back, "when he was here in '62."

"Won't be there. That one begins in the seventies." I could hear an empty metal pan set on a wooden table. "I'll get this batch into the oven. Hold on."

Photographs lined the hallway. History was imaged into every space. There was a brittle typewritten label "German Village of Hermannsburg" peeling away below a photograph. In the picture a brick steeple rises over the village, surrounded by pine forests. The fields are dotted with thatched huts, wooden barns and hayricks. There is heath and heather, sheep are grazing and bees are kept. Sifting into the picture frame, grains of sand had settled as ridges, like pink clouds above the land.

In their portraits the missionaries Schulze, Kempe and Hartwig look typecast: long beards and deeply set eyes, lips drawn, relentlessly severe. Their wives, even after fifteen years of living here, never altered the tightly wound hairstyles worn in their marriage portraits. And this was evidence of what? Had their *every* gesture been aimed at preparing the dark folk for the Second Coming?

The early Lutherans suffered through privation and drought, and more: the refusal of the natives to profess their sinful natures to the world. "We like fire," they had mocked, "Hell will be a good place." In a summary report to his board, Kempe wrote that, all things considered, "A mission under these circumstances could do no more than dig the Aborigines' graves."

Carl Strehlow, who succeeded Kempe, came to be regarded by the Aboriginal Elders as one of their own, "...one of those men of supreme authority," his son Theodore wrote. Theodore describes his father as having been the "rockplate" of life for the Hermannsburg Aboriginals. A rockplate, a repository of sacred knowledge, stored by the ancient ancestors for the benefit of those to come; this was no small tribute.

After his daily labors, Carl worked into the nights transcribing the notes on Aranda mythology and ritual he had made while talking with the old men. His work was published as *Die Aranda–Und Lorit-ja-Stämme in Zentral-Australia*, Frankfurt, 1907. "I have questioned the natives upon the point," wrote Carl of the benefits and responsibilities bound up with tjurunga ownership. In the section, *Die Tjurunga Der Aranda*, he relates one episode from the cusp of Aboriginal adulthood.

> When the novice has grown to a man his grandfather con-ducts him to the [hidden storehouse] where the tjurunga of his forefathers are kept, and shows them to him with the words: This is your body, this is your second self. If you take these tjurunga to another place, you will smart for it!

It was not clear to me when I read a translation of *Die Aranda* if, in Carl's time, the death penalty for mishandling tjurunga was being applied by the Aboriginal people. But the Aboriginal memory of executions was still vivid: "if ever a man showed a tjurunga to a woman, both of them were put to death," the pastor wrote. But, then, when the tjurunga are properly attended to, a man's "well-being is assured, guaranteed in fact." A man's tjurunga was his second self and was his forever. Considering Carl's success in gathering these objects for shipment to the Volker-museum, I wondered at how quickly the binding strictures seemed to have dissolved. The Lutherans, it looked to me, had found the lever to successfully rout the Opposition.

Walking toward me down the corridor, the baker wiped her hands on a towel, then tucked it into her belt. She was an Aboriginal woman of considerable age, still handsome, and dressed in boots and jeans like a country girl. She stopped beside me and tapped the glass of a picture frame.

"That's my mother there. In Freida Strehlow's sewing class." Her finger rested on a row of native women and several lanky girls, faces burnished and their hair slicked back. All wore identical ankle length, high-necked, full-sleeved dresses – Freida's own success at conversion? The baker shifted her glasses up the bridge of her nose and pointed to another photo. "That's the pipeline being laid, our first dependable water. For years the only water we had was brought in tanks by camel. The newcomers have no idea. They've always had water coming out the end of a tap. Let them live here for six years without rain and see what that does to them."

"You've been here for a while, then."

"I was born here and I'm eighty, so I've seen it all. I was a best friend of Helene, Pastor Albrecht's daughter." She meant Friedrich Wilhelm Albrecht, who took over the mission after Carl died. "That's the two of us there. Day by day we grew up together, and I loved Jesus like she did. When the missionaries left, I stayed. This is my country and I keep Jesus in it."

She led me into the Tea Room lounge where she set out another guest register, its leather binding dry and flaking. "Here you are, young man. Let's see if your dad left you a message." She asked me what had brought him out here. I told her of his oil interests while I turned pages that dated from the first of Pastor Albrecht's tenure. Here were names I recognized as fixtures of local history: Rex Batterbee, the Sydney artist who coached the Hermannsburg-born artist Albert Namitjira toward national prominence as a watercolorist; Theodore Strehlow; W.E. "Bill" Harney, the father of Bill Harney the Aboriginal storyteller; and eventually the missionary F. W. Albrecht, who was revisiting after his retirement: "Warmest thanks for kind hospitality on many occasions. Good-bye."

"My father was looking for oil west of here. Okay, there he is: 'W.J. Hafford, Namco Oil Exploration. November, 1962."

"Did he write a comment?"

"Yes. 'Permian shale!' He stopped here on his way back from the field, heading for Alice Springs. I'm Mark, by the way."

"Very pleased to meet you, Mark. Katrina." We shook hands. "Well, then. Is that all that brought you out here?"

"No, there is another matter. I don't know if I should talk openly about this. I mean, it's men's business, it concerns a sacred object."

"If you're talking about tjurunga stones, Mark, they don't mean a thing to me. Pastor Albrecht relieved us of that burden long ago. Look here." She led me to another photograph in the corridor. "See? That's me again, and that's Helene. We were just little girls then."

The picture's title was *Service at Manangananga Cave, October 1930*. Standing around the boulder-strewn mouth of a small cave was an Aboriginal congregation, well over a hundred people of all ages, dressed for church, and Pastor Albrecht at the cave's mouth.

"Where's this? What's going on?"

"It's down the Finke a little way. The cave is the old men's tjurunga storehouse. Or, it was until, let's see, seventy years ago."

"I thought those caves were strictly off-limits to women and children. What happened?"

"There's some who'll tell you the cave was assaulted, *pillaged*, by 'Christian soldiers.' But it wasn't like that. It was such a peaceful day. There are times in our lives we just don't forget. You can feel peace, Mark, just as you can feel fear."

"But...why? The missionaries before Albrecht must have been aware of the cave. Why did *he* challenge it?"

"Pastor Strehlow had been taken there, too, in his time, as an honored guest. Truth, Mark, he became..." and she hesitated, "indecisive. But Albrecht knew that it was time. Time at last for the men to decide between their tjurunga and Christ.

"You must understand, Mark, all around the mission in those days there were camps of half-wild people. There was mayhem. I know because I went back to my mum's camp every night. I saw heads split open. Oh, yes, Mark. Once an old man speared his wife just because she had been nagging him about a younger woman he wanted to marry. She died instantly. Well, that presented Albrecht with a dilemma, didn't it? The old man, by tribal law, was entitled to what he had done. But a line has to be drawn somewhere. Where would you draw the line, Mark? At polygamy? At murder?"

"And that's when he marched to the cave?"

"No. Albrecht said, 'There will be no more baptisms.' Can you imagine? No more baptisms! For the Christians that was very serious.

Their decision to empty Mananganga came from the men themselves. Well," she said, tapping her finger against the photograph, "Moses stood there before the cave..."

"Moses?"

"Moses Tjalkabota...and gave his famous sermon *Churinga or Christ*. Preached the lesson of the Golden Calf. Pastor Albrecht stood over the tjurunga stones the men had laid out on the ground. He called us children forward so we could touch them, to prove that they were powerless. Those stones were carried back here and lined up on that fence outside, harmless as dingo pelts for everyone to see. Now what did you want to ask me, Mark? Something about your father?"

"A tjurunga stone, from the mission. My father bought a tjurunga stone here and I want to find out where it came from. It's more than research. I'll give it back to the men who lost it. If they want it, of course."

She looked at me like that was the craziest thing she had ever heard. "Whatever for? Tjurunga, they were freely given up."

"I'm tempted to agree with you. But anyway, being given up doesn't mean they're not wanted back now."

"Well, you must do what you think is right, Mark. But consider this. When that mob from Yuendumu," she lifted her eyes toward the north, "went to the Adelaide museum and collected their tjurunga back again, what do you suppose happened? They brought them home and they were all pinched by the young men. Sold to tourists. Hopeless."

"Hopeless?"

"Yes, but I suppose not impossible to sort out. Did your father tell you where his came from?"

"No, that's the problem. He just said that he pulled it out of a camel bag at this mission. I thought someone here might know something."

"Pastor Albrecht did keep records of tjurunga that came into the mission. And he was here for thirty years before your dad arrived, so..."

"Can I see those? Do you have those records?"

"They're not here, Mark. They're in the archives. Four ledger books, I believe. I've got to finish, but I can look for them later on. I run the Tea Room kitchen and it's a very big weekend for Hermannsburg, you know. It's the one-hundred and twenty-fifth anniversary of the Mission. We'll be full up tomorrow, you can be sure. Can you come over to my house this evening? Ask anyone where the parsonage is." She tugged her headscarf taut and checked the knot in back.

"Katrina, just one other thing, please. I want to know what Hermannsburg was like when my father was here. Is there an old-timer in the community who would talk to me?"

"That would be Pastor Patrick. I'll ask Maria to take you over." She turned to wave at me. "Until, shall we say, five o'clock?"

Maria, a small woman but full of steam, burst through the doorway of the Strehlow House. She had a lot to do serving as a doctor at the town's clinic, as well as caring for her preschooler. And she was pitching in at the Tea Room for the anniversary weekend. She brushed past me with a quick "Come on, then" and lit off across the yard.

I followed her around the abandoned tannery just as two adolescents were squeezing out from between its loose sheet-iron panels, jars of petrol clutched in hand. Maria warned them off with a sternness Albrecht would admire, and they skulked drunkenly away.

Emerging through a gap in the precinct's fence, we entered a warren of cement-block houses. Barefoot youngsters played in the sandy lane, padding around among the remains of sun-bleached plastic toys. Two others chased a wheel rim from one of the several broken bicycles that lay about. A threadbare, deflated soccer ball landed with a *whomp* just behind me, source unknown.

Maria stopped at one of the houses where three women sat, legs outstretched in the sand, absorbed in a slow-moving card game. "Patrick," she demanded. "Is he here? This man wants to see him." She abruptly turned away and left me standing there.

At Hermannsburg, the benefit of "first love" for Christ clearly had long been spent. It occurred to me that for each of these women, enjoying her bit of shade, the Second Coming was not the one promised here for 125 years. It had come with the restoration of Aboriginal ownership of the ground she sat on. By and by, one of the women rose and went into the house.

Stubble-faced and bleary-eyed, Pastor Patrick stepped uncertainly into the sunlight. He had just been brought back from a bender in Alice Springs for the Mission's anniversary weekend. He was a small and gentle person, willing to oblige my questions. I also wanted to know if tjurunga still held any interest for the local men, but I dared not bring this up, at least not yet. He led me away from the women and the children, across the road and through the dust cloud raised by a delivery truck.

"These are my boys," he said of a half dozen adolescents playing basketball on the tarmac. Stepping away from me, he caught a ball bounced to him and threw it at the hoop, slowly warming up his aim. After a few more attempts he returned the ball and came back. We retired to a bench and watched the boys continue taking free throws.

He recalled how it was to grow up in Hermannsburg, although he was just a schoolboy when my father was here. He pointed to a large cross poking up from the highest hill beside the village. "Every Easter they used to put Easter eggs up on the hill with our names on em, see? Gotta go get right one."

"Like a tjurunga stone," I said. "Gotta get the right one." Patrick didn't seem to find this funny.

"Patrick, you're a Christian, a Lutheran?"

He replied, "Ummmm," suggesting *maybe*.

I asked, "The old religion, does it still exist here in Hermannsburg?" Patrick nodded.

"Were you raised at all in the traditional way, in the way of your father?"

"Yep."

"Initiated?"

"Yeah."

His candor, while not unrestrained, was more than I had any right to hope for. "What was it like?"

"Well, it's proper hard to go through. Gotta learn all about what the Aboriginal culture, what the Law is. How to respect em. Young ones can't get knowledge, only old ones, Elders."

"Are Aboriginal boys from here still initiated?"

"Yeah, still, every Christmas in the summer time. Can't initiate one at a time. Too much trouble."

"And the land, who owns this land, Patrick?"

Looking over his left shoulder he said, "Well, you know that, that's MacDonnell Range, where Namatjira mob is." Then looking to the right, "This one…James Range, I think. Oh, well, my mother's side is this Hermannsburg area and Palm Valley. And Gosse Bluff is my mother's side, too. My mother's father's area this side. My father's area that side, see?"

He had covered most all the land around us: 1500 square miles that had been deeded through an Aboriginal land trust, right up to the National Parks. "And what is your land?"

"Really…it's father's side. Ormiston Gorge area and right down to Ellery."

"It's a beautiful land. Do you like to leave town and go into your country?"

"Sometime I go out with watercolor and try to paint em from spot. I might be painting from photo. I got that…what you call that, it's a kind of camera? Take a picture, take em out?"

"Polaroid?"

"Umm. That kind. Yeah, it's good color, too, that one."

I told him why I had come to Hermannsburg, that I was looking for the source of the tjurunga my father had bought here. He asked me, "What country's it from?"

"Well," I sighed, "I don't know." Patrick smiled at that.

He told me, "They used to write this name on the back from where that story – you know, stories – which country it come from. Albrecht wrote that."

"Yes, Katrina from the Tea Room is going to show me his ledgers. Are tjurungas still used by the people?"

"There's a lot of people asking me to make fighting boomerang. I learned from the old people. You got to cut the right one, right kind of wood so your work will be easy."

I supposed that he misunderstood me, so I asked again if tjurunga have relevance today. He thought for a moment, then said, "There's some that my people there got a place where they can keep em. We got one. Just left it over there in the cave."

"I thought everyone here, the old men, gave those up. Why didn't your people hand this one over to the missionaries?"

"Old people didn't give that to Strehlow, not to Albrecht. They hided it away. My grandfather used to keep that one. Still here. Ours that Twin Boy totem rock. With that piece of rock and the Twin Boy mark on it, you holding the area. Like you own the mark, anyone can't take the land away from you."

"What land are you talking about?"

"Ntaria. This here."

"Patrick, do you mean that your grandfather's tjurunga stone says your family owns Hermannsburg? Did you inherit this land along with his tjurunga?"

"Um hmm. Not this town yet. Palm Valley, down the Finke. That judge, he looked on that stone and said that, two years ago. Long time we knew that already."

"Well, what does the tjurunga say on it? How did the judge know – I mean, did he think it was a map or something like a legal deed?"

"Just got the mark for this Hermannsburg and Palm Valley. It's called Twin Boys. That story is Twin Boy Dreaming. They all in that rock."

"And that's all it takes to satisfy the government?"

"Umm...you got to know the stories, you got to know the Dreaming. I been lookin after that country with my people and all."

"There's gas or oil out there in Palm Valley, right?"

"That's not ours. But that valley, he got water, all the times water. Good tucker, too."

"What tucker, Patrick?"

121

"Oh, they got that women tucker. Witchetty grub and that bush tomato. They got fig and wild banana, onion, plum, too. Got fish. Got...woman get that bush medicine."

"Sounds like a paradise."

"Got tobacco."

"And now you own all that..."

"They call it...what that?... *Land Rights*. We share control with Parks people. Gas goes to another. I got that judge's report. You want to see em?"

I followed Patrick back to his house. I wanted to know how a judge worked out a title to land through an engraved stone. Patrick brought out a sand-encrusted government report that he had been using to sheave his watercolors. He slid them out and gave me the document, afterwards excusing himself to rest a little from his "cold." I returned to the bench and went through what the judge had handed down.

Following two hundred years of colonial occupation the federal government in the early nineteen-eighties allowed that the Aboriginal population had some legitimate claim to their country. Eventually, half of Northern Territory, an immense amount of land owned by the Crown, came under the control of Aboriginal "Land Trusts." A clan, the traditional constitutional unit, was then able to make an exclusive claim for a section based on primary spiritual responsibility. Among the last petitions to be filed, as the window of opportunity was closing, was the Palm Valley Land Claim, presented at a hearing in 1995.

Palm Valley is a small National Park renowned for the majestic red rock handiwork of the Finke River. As Patrick suggested, it is a relic of Eden. Its waters provide a refuge for one-quarter of the plant species in Central Australia, some surviving from an ancient, more hospitable climatic era. Among the benefits at stake in the Claim was more than just the privilege of foraging the natural tucker; there were also perpetual rights to future mineral development. Palm Valley gas keeps the lights on both in Alice Springs and Darwin.

The Palm Valley Land Claim, as Patrick's report spelled out, was submitted against the Crown by two competing claimants, each a clan residing in Hermannsburg, and both with deep genealogical roots. Justice Gray presided, and it was he who would ultimately decide who was in and who was out. In earlier days such a dispute would be settled with a split skull. Instead, Gray intended to filter through modern jurisprudence ancient Aboriginal kinship systems, principles of descent, models of land tenure, provable spiritual affiliation – in his words, reams of "tedious imponderabilia." Ultimately, Gray visited Palm Valley's sacred sites with men from each of the claimant groups, noting the distinct and occasionally overlapping mythologies. He listened to their chanting, observed ritual performances and scrutinized the telling of their stories.

Initially, the claims of either side appeared equally valid. "It is impossible for me to express a view," wrote Justice Gray, "as to which version of each dreaming story is the 'orthodox' version, if such a version even exists."

Ultimately, the court's judgment gave Pastor Patrick's clan their hoped for freehold on the paradisal Palm Valley. The deciding factor was Patrick's grandfather's tjurunga. Yet, even though Patrick believed that with his Twin Boy tjurunga no one could take his land away, an appeal was still possible. A superior tjurunga could reverse Gray's ruling in favor of the clan that had lost out, the Njalkas. The final resolution hinged on a decision yet to be made by a museum seven hundred miles away in Melbourne.

Gus Williams headed the Njalka clan. I knew him first as the person who had invited me to ride in on the mail van. Meeting him, I found a rather imposing man, large of girth and topped off with a cream-colored Stetson. In his office, he kept a guitar within reach and was obviously comfortable in his role as Ntaria Council president.

The competition for rights between the clans had begun early, even before the Lutherans arrived in Hermannsburg. But it erupted after they left, when the Williams family took on the task of managing the town. If the family had saved the community from chaos, they also had invested themselves in Council jobs. Gus was a high-stakes gambler; after twenty years of holding things together in Hermannsburg, he was now prepared to re-engage Patrick's Renkaraka/Ratara clan even though losing his appeal might mean having to pack up and leave town.

Gus was bitter about a lot of things, beginning with the Lutherans. "They stole our culture from us and broke our sacred objects. They've destroyed everything we held sacred." But, he confided to me, "There's a few objects coming back. I'm getting one back soon."

Melbourne's Museum Victoria had hired an anthropologist to trace the provenance of its tjurunga collection. While cross-referencing records of the collecting ethnologists to current genealogies he produced a perfect match: one tjurunga stone and Gus's great grandfather. The stone had a name: *The Thunderbolt*.

The Thunderbolt was "discovered" in 1930 near Hermannsburg, where the mythological personage of Kantjira commanded the atmosphere: the high-altitude glow of sheet lightning, the throwing of thunderbolts, and the frequency of rainfall. The story of Kantjira's titanic battle with another "big rain-man," along with other associated legends, were all recorded by Pastor Strehlow at the Hermannsburg Mission before the stone was carried away. The object passed through private hands, appeared in ethnological literature and was obtained by the Dupont Collection. Eventually it came back to Australia and entered the holdings of the Museum Victoria, and this is where the anthropologist rediscovered it.

The anthropologist had counseled the museum that The Thunderbolt, as a territorial spoil, should go to Pastor Patrick's family, the current victors in the Palm Valley claim. But another consultant, unaware of the dynamics of the land claim just concluded, casually approached Gus with the news of his impending windfall. "It's recorded and written in the white man's language," Gus told me, "that there's a sacred object belonging to my great grandfather."

If the tjurunga came into Gus's hands, the Njalka clan would undoubtedly reassert their right to Palm Valley's resources and as critically, maintain family control of the township's council – in, or perhaps out of, court. "Gus doesn't have any rights. No rights," was the assessment later offered to me by Grant Parker who was superintendent of the mission after Pastor Albrecht left, and he had 40 years experience to back him up. What would happen, I asked Parker, should The Thunderbolt go back to one clan or the other at Hermannsburg? His reply: "Someone is going to get killed."

I left Patrick's report in the care of the women still playing cards outside his house and headed where their wagging hands directed me, across the village toward Pastor Albrecht's former parsonage.

Resplendent fuchsia-colored bougainvillea cascaded from the top of a barbed wire fence, almost engulfing the gate whose lock hung open on its chain. I passed through and went into the yard. The enclosure held the faint, oily smell of citrus but otherwise was dry as cinders. Water drip, dripped from a crack in the decayed garden hose, creating a little oasis from which bathing birds darted as I approached.

Katrina stepped out to greet me and to show me around the yard. In one corner was the pastor's "orchard," an ash heap strewn with charred tin cans, and the source of the citrus fragrance – a lemon tree densely hung with fruit. She stopped under the naked wires of a grape arbor to name the fruit of Albrecht's labor. "There were eight varieties of grape: lady's finger, sultana, crystal and five others. Back there are the fig and mulberry trees. They do need pruning." To me, they looked beyond all hope. But "with love and attention," she assured me, "they'll return." As she stood there, with her hands on hips, Katrina radiated joy. She delighted in this vision of rebirth although any effort she might have made toward realizing it was stalled. "There's a cross in the birdcage," Katrina chirped as we passed by it. "Isn't that cute?"

She stopped in the kitchen and lifted her kettle up to the spout. Any water in her catchment tank was a year old if a day. "How do you like your tea, Mark?"

With water purification tablets, I thought. "With lemon, please," I said.

She pointed into the next room. "The books you want are in there, on the parlor table." The windows were shuttered and draped, keeping the coolness and the dark inside. The room seemed to hold its breath. A low-wattage bulb hung above four folio-sized ledgers: hardbound with leatherette corner tabs, tall pages ruled in faint blue lines. I settled myself into a chair, set my tjurunga on the table and opened up my Moleskine alongside.

Albrecht had entered one hundred seventeen lots of tjurunga, two hundred and twenty individual stones in all. He devoted two full pages to each entry, all beginning alike with three facts: the tjurunga's totemic affiliation, the clan allied with that totem, and a place name for the sanctuary where that tjurunga was once kept. All the stones were hastily sketched: an ink loop encircling its unique set of engraved icons, and each icon – chevron, dot, concentric circle, wavy line – was called out for the feature it represented in myth.

On the opposite page was the tjurunga itself. The actual stone had been laid underneath, and the paper rubbed hard with black crayon so that, from behind storm clouds of broad gray strokes the recessed icons flashed white like lightning. Beginning at the bottom of the page, and continuing as needed onto the next, was narrated the segment of a mythological story that the stone and its icons represented.

Finally, scrawled in pencil across each entry was the name of the visitor who purchased the object from the mission and what was paid for it, never more than a few shillings.

My immediate task was to match my tjurunga with a rubbing, with its rubbing; it would register exactly under its page, unique as a fingerprint, mating their designs, their whorl.

Turning the pages, I watched for my tjurunga's most recognizable feature, the concentric circle motif, a code that would pass me into the center of its meaning.

The concentric circle appeared page after page after page and, according to Albrecht's notes, represented any number of things: a totemic caterpillar's hole in the ground, a camping place, emu droppings, honey ant burrows or birds' nests, a man's navel or an old maid's womb, even the entrails of a wild turkey. These icons, the briefest of notations, merely hinted at the complexities of myth, myth that only sensuous contact, tribal memory and storytelling could fill out.

Putting my pencil down, I discovered a cup of tea on the table to my left. It was no longer hot, but lively with a perfect spike of lemon.

I could hear fat spitting in a skillet and Katrina humming while she prepared her dinner. Peeking through the shutters, I discovered it was night. The time had passed so quickly.

I slowed down while going through the second ledger, pausing to read Albrecht's transcriptions of the myths surrendered with each tjurunga. I realized that I would never again see anything like Albrecht's ledgers. They gave a privileged glimpse of the details of religious convictions elsewhere kept from outsiders. These were my gateway into an exotic sphere, my entrée into humanity's oldest and longest running mythological drama.

The myths often began with a pursuit between some totemic creatures, ending in a wash of blood revenge. The protagonists set off after trespassers or kidnappers or assassins with all the magical powers available to them. If their pursuits from time to time were righteous, just as often blood flowed from victims of mistaken identity. I saw no morals being transmitted, no canon of lessons being proposed. Nothing in Aboriginal life had been left out. Everything, poetic or poisonous, vile or virtuous, painful or pleasurable, found its place inside some story. It was, from a moral point of view, an unsatisfying smear of human folly. I put the ledger down, sat upright, stretched out my arms, and then slumped back into place.

In the third ledger, I found episodes of magic among the Dreaming stories: a tree thickly hung with tjurunga bearing a clan of fully initiated men, and sorcery: the deadly effect of an assassin's pointing bone. And there were histories of how knowledge was brought to the people. The myths depicted keenly observed habits of wildlife: how the night bird, in pursuit of his prey, hunted for flies in starlight, and of the honey ant's attraction to the sweetness of Mulga-tree blossoms. In this I saw a perfection; the creatures' habits appeared to be the schema for the ancestors' journeys, and those had evolved into the mortal Aboriginals' ritual walkabout. The habit of a creature was not a metaphor, but a man's source of understanding the cosmic order. Following the way of these patterns allowed him to fulfill his existence.

The myths unfailingly and abruptly ended as the totemic characters tired, entered a cave, and each turned into a stone tjurunga.

Pastor Albrecht meticulously recorded all these curious features of the Dreamtime matter-of-factly and perhaps without discernment; he was not an ethnologist-collector in the Strehlow mold. He was a dealer in artifacts, authenticating every object, not incidentally in expectation of the highest possible return.

Albrecht's translating the Bible into native dialect made some sense, however perverse, but reducing Arandic oral cosmology into script was a different matter altogether. His strings of written words could no more evoke the Aboriginal lived experience than the reductive icons engraved on a tjurunga could cause the stone to speak aloud. Nothing had been preserved in Albrecht's tjurunga stories. They were an affliction. In receiving the sacred objects, in writing the myths down, he had hurried the land toward silence. He had participated in the murder of myth.

Nearing the end of the fourth ledger, I came upon an account of a matched pair of tjurunga, one for a man and the other his little boy. Their shared myth story ended with them side by side for eternity, turned into "Tj." stones. The entry also contained an account of the tjurunga stones' separation by theft. Although set down plainly as Albrecht had done for every other object, both the myth and the actual history of these two stones affected me particularly.

> An old man named Arabi, once showed some white people, the first that came here with camels, into the cave. They took a number of other Tj. for which they deposited new Tomahawks and new butcher knives. But this Tj. [the second one later presented to Albrecht] they missed and didn't find it.

The initial plundering of the cave at Karkilja Kilja had been committed by a white man acting out of ignorance, or disregard, of the consequences. The second tjurunga, left undiscovered, was later removed by an Aboriginal, taken to the mission and eventually sold by Albrecht for seven shillings. This latter removal presented a problem. Had it been owned by the man who took it? What was his intention in handing it over to Albrecht? Was he threatened, did he gain, and how would that affect any rights his descendants may have had to reclaim it later?

The tjurunga caves, scattered in hills and valleys all around the mission, had been emptied on behalf of people like my father, visitors who carried cash. Everyone was implicated, I groused to myself: the tourists, the missionaries, and the Aboriginals who had plundered their own caves. Whenever accounts of tjurunga theft were portrayed in the Dreaming stories, the pilfering never passed without some immediate retribution. In our less ideal time, the same could not be said.

Now I knew this man *Albrecht* who had been named in the Museum of Cultures's new Aboriginal Gallery. I closed my eyes and recalled a recorded voice I had heard playing: "How come that bloke Albrecht wants to break our Law, very important Law. It's all tied together, with the land, and the tjurunga. The Law is all one piece, can't take a part out. Otherwise it will fall down." I weighed that "house of cards" lament against Baldwin Spencer's assurance from way back: "When the tjurunga that had been lost are in hand once more, the Dreamtime will again spring to life."

That was not going to happen here today. I had done my best to satisfy my father's conscience and an Aboriginal's claim on this tjurunga. For two weeks I had tramped over the countryside not knowing what was revered and what was common stone, what was sacred myth and what was humbug. I had no confidence that another day would make any difference either to my comprehension or for resolving the tjurunga's proper placement.

There was longer any doubt about how I would dispose of my dad's thin bit of indeterminate stone. Pickering said to me at the museum that short of a proper return to the Centre, I should "fling it into the sand." That is what I would do tomorrow. Then I would call Allen from Alice Springs to tell him I was on my way to Cairns and the Barrier Reef.

Meanwhile, Hermannsburg's population of five hundred souls had swelled fourfold with the influx of Lutherans for the mission's anniversary weekend. The village was astir. I walked to my campground alongside a stream of out-of-state cars released from the alcohol check-point, their headlights boring a tunnel through the dust.

This was a big town for western music, and Gus Williams was a picker himself, but I couldn't tell on which side of the road he was that night – in the field of dark figures dancing up a fury, or with the cluster of Lutherans gathered under the mission chapel's new illuminated cross.

Groups of barefoot children wearing soccer shorts and sports jerseys walked arm in arm alongside me, laughing and teasing each other. It felt like a night at the county fairs I had known in the Texas of my youth, even more so when skyrockets were launched; they latticed the night beneath a half-full moon.

17

I SLEPT a dense, senseless sleep and crawled from my tent next morning to the day's bright prospect. The terminal event of my Australian venture was finally at hand. I breakfasted outside the campground manager's trailer with my coffee and the donut he offered me, and we listened together to his radio. A dialogue was being broadcast live on the Christian Network from just down the road, at the mission precinct. The interviewer said, "I understand, Reverend, that Aboriginal people across Australia are searching for ways to embrace Christ without sacrificing their traditional core beliefs. I'm sure you know their proposal: *In the Beginning was the Rainbow Serpent. And the Rainbow Serpent was with God, and God was with the....*" The manager snapped off his radio.

"See what we have to put up with here?"

The broadcast was finished by the time I entered the precinct. A crewman was coiling up cables from around the broadcast booth – a card table in the shade of a gum tree, laden with electronics. Nearby, an Aboriginal man was bending the interviewer's ear as though he needed to entrust the man with one last, essential message. "Christ got his totem, too. That's us. We're *Christ's* totem here in the Centre."

The Lutherans were gathered outside in the mission yard for the anniversary weekend's main event, the worship service. Seated in rows of camp chairs, the ladies wore bonnets and the men straw hats or caps against the morning's already hot sun. Under whatever scraggly shade the compound's perimeter offered, the Aboriginal congregation settled onto the ground. A flatbed trailer served as an altar, and a brass-handled wooden traveling case of the Lord's Supper was open on a lace-draped table. Behind the chapel, cook stoves were being fired up and griddles greased.

Hymns were raised. "What a Friend We Have in Jesus" came from an English choir on my right and was sung simultaneously in Aranda on my left.

> *What a friend we have in Jesus,* Tjina nurnaka Jesuala,
> *All our sins and griefs to bear!* Korna nurnak' iwuma!

The day became sweltering as the service progressed, the Lutherans daubing their brows and disturbing the flies that wished to drink there. To deliver the homily, the President of the Lutheran Church in Adelaide rose from his chair on the trailer and approached the microphone. His sermon was taken from Isaiah 35: 6b-7a. The text seemed custom made for the residents of this desert.

> For waters shall break forth in the wilderness,
> and streams in the desert;
> the burning sand shall become a pool,
> and the thirsty ground springs of water…

He asked, "Is the faith of our Holy Fathers *just another trick*? No. It is God's voice speaking. All that the desert needs, all that *our lives* need, is the refreshing water, the water that flows from the side of Jesus Christ. Our lives will no longer be blown about without meaning…"

And a sudden wind arose, a mighty gust from the far end of the compound. Bending the branches of the gum tree overhead, it swept the podium, blowing the minister's white hair over his forehead and making a pennant of his shawl. The cloud of dust that it had lifted then fell and spread over the damp, upturned faces, a blessing by the desert.

The speaker withdrew and an invitation was made for the congregation to partake of Communion. As the whites rose, so rose their dark-skinned brethren who, having caught the scent of grilling meat carried over the chapel's roof, walked around the queue forming for the sacraments, to the far side of the chapel, and lined up at the griddle. I joined them there for a sausage sandwich.

I returned to the Tea Room, bought a foil-wrapped strudel and put it with a bottle of water on top of my tjurunga stone, the perennial ballast at the bottom of my satchel. I took the path leading down the bluff toward the Finke River, to select my stone's final resting place.

The Finke River was all but dry, basically a sand corridor winding between stunted hills, and overflown by the circuits of high-gliding buzzards. I walked with *The Songlines* open before me, turning the final few pages while my feet found their way over the loose surface. Because my path and Chatwin's had been overlapping ever since I arrived in the Centre, it was no surprise that his final chapter put him in this riverbed, giving a lift to an Aboriginal man en route to his tjurunga cave. *The Songlines* concludes with a cascade of entertaining vignettes and quotations on the subject of man's eternal need to move along. Among these I found one that suited my frame of mind: *Solvitur ambulando* – it is solved by walking. I closed the book, withdrew my attention from the scenery and bowed my head to watch the river stones pass underfoot.

After a while, and for no evident reason, I stopped walking and raised my head. The channel had turned south and was now walled in by steep outcrops of stone stained an oxblood red. These palisades were cut through with tributary canyons that receded into tangles of spindly trees and blue-green shrubs, and out of which the songs of birds occasionally echoed. Massive stone blocks had calved off the cliff faces, landing on the sand, and been knocked into bricks. These had been run downriver by the roughhousing of summer floods, their bloody patina rubbed off, and were rendered into rose-hued cobbles by the billions.

A stand of stout river gums grew mid-stream, survivors of the river's violence. Corpses of trees that had been uprooted gathered against their trunks, and, just behind this barricade, on the riverbed, was a peninsula of white sand. A breeze bowed down pale yellow grasses that, in gently sweeping arcs, wrote calligraphy onto the sand's fine-grained surface. Through the grass stalks air whispered a wordless sermon. This is where the tjurunga would stay; I would leave it here in this riverbed among its fellow stones.

At the trickling of the stream, I dropped to my knees and reached my hands out over the sun-warmed water. I pulled a heap of stones toward me, leaving a shallow trough where the water pooled. Then I lifted the tjurunga from my bag and gently placed it into this bath among the others. My stone looked the part, although arrayed in a finer tunic.

If I forced my eyes out of focus, the surface engravings disappeared, and the tjurunga was lost in the sameness all around it. Then it would snap back into its ordained distinctiveness, resisting submersion into the order from which it had long ago been lifted. It had been ascribed properties of life and, perhaps for centuries, satisfied the men who venerated it. Yet, lying here unprotected for a single season, it would be scoured by the Finke, defrocked like a bogus pope, no matter if the spirit inside the stone might remain.

I upended my rucksack, tumbling out the wadded tinfoil of my strudel, the water bottle I so wanted at this moment, and my Moleskine. Thumbing the little black notebook given to me a short while ago in Dallas, I found few pages still unmarked.

In Alice Springs I had introduced myself to Frank Lassinger, the son of a mission stockman and now a prominent naturalist. I told him I was a fan of Chatwin, assuming that Chatwin had become the town's adopted favorite son. I was wrong. Lassinger warned me off. "You can't write about Aboriginal peoples unless you put in your time. Chatwin was here for *five minutes*! You've either got to give them years of engagement," he told me close to my face, "or stay the hell out."

I opened my notes and skimmed the pages. What had I meant by this: "Mt. Liebig: subjective impressions of likely area on basis of observations of items on the post" or "body painting and object painting precede wall art evidenced by location of ochre"? Why had I thought "trance said to be first accompanied by simple geometric visions" was important, or even useful?

I closed my Moleskine, coiled my arm and flung the little pad across the stones. The pages fluttered once in protest, and were gone.

I lay face down, my eyes too close to the riverbed to focus, and peered into the shadowed space between the stones. I felt empty, and I was not sure why. It wasn't about the tjurunga or the crumbled edifice of Aboriginal spirituality or really about anything else I had learned or come into contact with on this odd quest. But something essential was missing, something within myself, and I didn't know what could be done about it.

I might have lain in this manner indefinitely, accompanied by flies and misgivings, if a car hadn't come along. I could hear it laboring at a distance as it made its way over the shifting bed of stone and sand. When it came into view I saw that it was a bright, clean, late model four-wheeler, its single occupant behind the pleasant isolation of closed windows. I thought, the driver must be heading downriver toward Palm Valley, and as quickly as I could I jumped up and shot out my hand, my thumb extended for a ride.

I had forgotten how fine a thing air conditioning can be and how agreeably picturesque a country becomes when framed by a window. He leaned backward out of the day's glare, jerked the steering left and right trying to stay in the shallows and rocking us back and forth, shoulder to shoulder. Men's cologne – it had been years. Terry, he said his name was Terry. He wore his thinning hair slicked back, and his short-shorts tight so his thighs swelled outside the hem and his crotch bulged.

"You've got a beaut," Terry said glancing at my lap. Oh, god, I thought. This is just my luck.

"How'd you get that?" Still glistening from its dip like a fish just landed, the tjurunga lay soaked over my trousers.

"I...I picked it up in the riverbed."

"That's rare. Washed out of the hills? You could sell that, you know. It's a tjurunga stone."

But I left it behind, I was sure I had left it behind. This had to be some trick. I slid my fingers under its edges and lifted it an inch.

Terry just went on, "...not all worth the same, see. Some are unique, some duplicates. But the best, the really old ones, love to deal with one of those." He grabbed another look at my stone. "A real looker. Found it, did you? Right there, where I picked you up? Lying in the stream?"

"It's not stolen, if that's what you're thinking. Not by me anyway."

"No worries, mate. Nothing intended. Keep me in mind, though." One hand whipped a business card from his shirt pocket then clamped back on the wheel: "Red Centre Art and Artefacts. Canberra. Melbourne. Sydney."

I lay the tjurunga on the floor and out of view. The car veered from edge to edge, riding the trough like a raft at sea. "Few years ago," Terry said, "Sotheby's sold one like yours. Brought five times the price of other, in my opinion, equally handsome Aboriginal objects on offer. More'n any Oceania in the catalog. Except, as I recall, a Maori canoe prow and an Easter Island deity figure, of which there are possibly only five. Stunning little statue that was, too."

"Who bought it, the tjurunga?"

Terry shrugged his shoulders. "Someone looking for high spiritual value rather than being put off by that quality." He gunned the motor on a straightaway. "Think of the delicious pleasure. Possessing something so completely prized and sorely missed."

"They knew, then, where it came from."

"Mereenie Bluff Ranges, just west of Hermannsburg. Annotation by a Reverend Albrecht. The Dreaming figures, sacred sites, all named. CLC put up twenty thousand by proxy. Not enough by half."

"Central Land Council, you mean to say. Alice Springs, right?"

"Recently spent a million dollars for a portion of the Strehlow collection of tjurunga, intending to distribute the lot. Keep an eye on overseas auction houses, they do. Their lawyers are quite skilled at making their perspective known."

"They're bringing tjurunga back to Australia, then."

"Once they're here, they stay. Legislated Federal priority. Just like the early canvases from Papunya. Sacred designs. Secret."

"Papunya."

"Settlement outside Alice Springs. See that in the boot? The carton of boomerangs and wastebaskets? All brightly painted up with *sacred designs*. Yeah, but the early days... Papunya paintings from back then, extremely tradable. Very few on the loose now." He jerked his thumb behind at a bundle of canvas, rolled and tied. "I send em jpegs my clients want reproduced. These chaps in Papunya, the old timers, Dinny, Old Albert, Paddy Carroll and them, their new work fetches very well, internationally, mind you." Terry lifted his foot from the accelerator, and we glided into a parking slot at the edge of a scummy pond, a grove of cycads half scorched by wildfire. "Anyhow, that stone at your feet, that's the original canvas. All the new acrylic crap is very bright and colorful. They're a gloss, as a pamphlet is to the Word of God. But bless me, how they sell."

18

ROBBIE STOPPED the Ntaria mail van at the far edge of Alice Springs, let me out and made a U-turn for the Post Office. In front of me was an unattractive cinderblock building, its glass door lettered "Central Land Council" and beneath that were the words, "The Land Is Always Alive."

I told the receptionist that I had a tjurunga stone to give over. She left her desk for the back office, and a moment later a young man stepped out. "I'm David. Just leave your things here. Let's go for a coffee. Have a chat."

The Silver Bullet Café & Art Gallery is backed onto a steep hill, a Caterpillar Dreaming site, flanked on the left by the Desert Tracks Tyre Store, and a truck welding operation on the right. The café itself, a sixty-foot aluminum trailer, was open for business.

On its patio men and women, townies and bushies, lawyers, anthropologists and government policy gadflies, shod in dusty boots or flip-flops, sipped mint iced tea under broad-brimmed hats. They leaned toward each other chatting earnestly about the complications of land rights and compensation, the town's alcohol problem, and native language as *the* essential element for cultural regeneration. There was also frequent reference to "going bush": having just *been bush*, or being ready at any time to *go bush*.

Inside the trailer the waitress behind the pie-case waved us toward the only vacant table. David sat back to massage his eyes. I held up my menu and pointed to item three: the butterflied, lemon grilled prawn with avocado stuffed croissant. I was famished. And it's never too early for pie.

Mike, the founder of the Silver Bullet, was passing among the tables patting shoulders. He leaned on my chair's backrest to address David, reporting that despite having on the property a tin-roofed, field-stone-chimney structure built in 1943, something left behind by the 9th Australian Advanced Army Ordnance Corp, the cafe had failed to qualify as a National Historic Landmark. But Mike was pleased to announce that it had just been put on the National Register of Oddly Significant Places. "Cheers, mate," said David, hoisting his coffee mug. "Well done."

David was in no hurry to jump into my business so he told me something about himself. He was twenty-seven. As a student in Adelaide he had disappointed his parents by abandoning his conservatory lessons and taking up studies in anthropology, eventually entering that field through the widest possible gate, in service to the Aboriginals.

Nothing in David's temperament suited him especially well for his work. He spoke with great deliberateness – not from any lassitude of mind, but out of impatience with the tangled codes inherent to words. Learning Aboriginal dialects and something of their concepts of eternity had induced a stuttering speech, as a chile pepper might bring on the hiccups. After weeks out bush negotiating contracts between Aboriginal landholders and mining companies, he would come home, drop the blinds and listen to Buxtehude into the night with the volume up loud.

It was while squatting for hours, sweltering under awnings in some remote settlement with a sheaf of contract drafts at his side, waiting for one party or another to show up, that women unrolled their paintings on the ground before him. He wasn't buying but had questions about their stories, and the circles, lines and dots employed to tell them. His persistent curiosity drew in the older men who, over time, became less evasive, more forthcoming. They admitted that only fragments of the sacred designs were nowadays remembered, enough to make a convincing painting, but that authoritative knowledge of the myths was now denied them due to the historical loss of their tjurunga stones, their mnemonic texts.

David was struck by their dilemma. He thought about these things on long drives between appointments. He put it to me this way: "Without the assurance of this mode of experience, the native moral code cannot be effectively learned, its forces cannot be internalized. Without their tjurunga, there will only be c-c-contracts for land use."

From his point of view, no tjurunga should be left out on the loose, and certainly not in the hands of any white man. He thought that one day perhaps he might help an itinerant stone find its way back home.

"If you'd be willing to give me some time with this.... You hang on to the stone. All I want is a photograph. Let me make a Xerox. And you're in luck on one count. Max is in today."

"Max?" The Max I had met at the Rock Art Congress closing event, who was working to help his people to be human? "Yes," he said. And he was now the Land Council's go-to man for facilitating the return of all tjurunga. As an acknowledged Law man, Max had traveled to museums in Adelaide, Melbourne, and Sydney, negotiating for the release of sacred objects. As chair of the Central Land Council he had written in his first annual report, "We need them back home so that we can put the young ones through our kindergarten and the older they get, they will learn more in the culture." This motive, the return of sacred objects, became a pillar of the Land Council's statutory mission.

"Call me," said David. "Four o'clock? We'll see what he's had to say."

I called David from a pay phone, my bags tangled at my feet, my flight onward to Cairns not yet booked.

"I showed Max the Xerox," David told me. "His initial reaction, the object would have come from an area northwest of Alice Springs, maybe somewhere between Mount Zeil and Yayayi. His recommendation was that I discuss the photo with senior men in Papunya. That's a community with a rich cultural constituency, a bush network."

"Tomorrow? Can we go there tomorrow?"

"A bit early for you yet, I'd say. These blokes might feel uncomfortable." Silence.

"I was sort of on my way out..." I said.

"All I can offer you at this point, Mark, is that if the Elders are prepared to *look* at the photo, and *consider* receiving the object, then I'm sure they would be delighted to meet you and extend their regards."

David would be able to stop at Papunya on his return from Kintore. He would radio his office and leave a message for me. Could I wait a day or two?

I could stay another week if it would help, but that was all. That was my limit. Classes at the community college would soon be starting up again and my students were expecting me. My flight out of the country was already booked for the eighth day: Qantas ADL to SYD to LAX to NYC, then home, PVD.

Karla's number was in the phone book. Her housemate Angela answered, "She's got a group on tour just now, but no worries, Mark. I know who you are and I'm sure she'll be pleased to have you."

In their living room that night, I sat on the edge of my sofa bed and drew a grid for a seven-day calendar, accounting for all the time I had at my disposal.

Each evening I would sit under the tree in her yard, smoke a cigarette and then cross out another day. When I had filled the sixth box, it would be time to give up and go back to Adelaide.

I put an X through the first day on my calendar.

The manager at Jiramba Gallery, a mobile pressed to his ear, paced around unframed canvases stacked on the floor like carpets in an Arab bazaar. "New production's been very slow lately," he told his client. "There's this bloke, a dealer from Sydney, who's been buying them in lots. No, he orders over the email. I've given them a lot of canvas but my last trip out I brought back just two small works. I was quite disappointed." The manager clicked off, hauled in his sidewalk advert board, and closed shop for his afternoon cuppa.

Yes, he said, artists from Papunya occasionally come by asking for "grub money" but, with no new paintings on offer, they're routinely turned away. "Might be one or two in town. Check the river. Ask around for Old Albert by name. His people's section would be up there." He pointed around the far side of Anzac Hill.

The Todd's riverbed was in evacuation mode. A police jeep drove along the adjacent sidewalk, a bullhorn bellowing: "Get out now." And the people minded. Women and men scampered from their camps in twos and fives carrying cartons, blankets, and cookware. Where possessions were dropped, they were abandoned. Once safe on the bank, the river dwellers stood smoking and chattering and waiting for the flood to arrive. I walked along asking from group to group, "Old Albert? Old Albert?" but barely turned a single head.

I had witnessed a flash flood once before in desert Texas. At its onset, the sound was the rumble of distant thunder. Then it became a physical sensation as boulders were rolled down and bashed along the riverbed. When the rising river came, it came as riotous applause, wave slapping wave, the water deepening and widening, intent, it seemed, on leveling everything. But on the Todd it was different. A frothy chocolate-colored tongue of water appeared, nudging ahead a mat of debris. It made only the hissing sound of water percolating into sand. But women shrieked and children ran and skipped alongside like it was a circus on parade. The surge was soon spent, sucked down into the sand. The river camps were reoccupied. No Old Albert had stepped forward.

Upriver, the sidewalk became a footpath winding among boulder fields. Before heading back, when turning round for a last visual sweep, my gaze fell on another citizen of the land, a Black-footed Rock Wallaby perched atop a big stone jumble, staring down at me.

I shouted up at her, "Old Albert?"

"Albert," echoed down.

There was a three-quarter moon, like a piece of quickly ripening fruit, hanging nearly in my hand.

The gal at the Council office told me that David had radioed in. Before reaching Kintore, he was halted by deep, sucking mud on the track. He would camp the night and report again tomorrow. Meanwhile, Karla was still away with her tour group.

I crossed out the second day on my calendar.

On the top floor of the Strehlow Research Centre, at the apex of the spiral form in which it was built, is a heavy door and next to it an intercom. In this laid back town called Alice, which lifts its skirts for any tourist passing through, the SRC was the most locked down place I had encountered. I stated my name and asked if I might speak with the director. I was still peeved at him for squelching Murry's plan to hand back my tjurunga at the Rock Art Congress. It would have been so easy, saved me all this trouble.

Sequestered beyond the door was the raw material of Strehlow's ethnology, the things he had collected: sacred objects, sacred songs, photographs and motion pictures of sacred ceremonies, and the 44 field diaries he made over forty-two years. Much of this had been seized, taken from his home by the State after his death.

I was studying the display of Strehlow's photographic equipment – a 4X5 inch glass plate Graphlex with a Leitz f/3.5 lens and a Bolex H16s movie camera – when the office door opened. A tall man with a hedge of auburn hair and a broad smile reached out his hand. "Mark? I'm Brett. Please, come on in. I think I know why you're here."

I followed him to his office, and he invited me to sit down on the couch. Brett's walls were decorated with framed reproductions of Strehlow's photographs and several taped-up crayon doodles and finger paintings made by his daughter.

He closed the door and settled behind his desk. For a moment he pressed his steepled fingers against his lips, watching me, then spoke. "This is not a personal indictment, Mark," he said, "but if you had proceeded with your tjurunga's hand-over as planned it would have seemed, at best, gratuitous, even patronizing and, at worst, it might have caused a great offense."

I said, "I was told, and I believe, that it is very important to get tjurunga stones back into the right hands. Now I've heard that you've got a thousand sacred objects here…"

"Twelve hundred."

"…and they've been locked up in the middle of their homeland for a decade. That's incomprehensible to me. I have this image of all these tjurunga in an adjacent room like books in a library that are written in a language that will be indecipherable within a generation."

"Your image, Mark, is very colorful."

"Your organization considers itself an arbiter in repatriation matters, but isn't that just another form of paternalism, an attitude handed down from colonial days?"

"Your point is well taken, Mark, but no. Arbitration is simply not our purview. We would not want to be in a position where we're seen as having recognized one person's rights over another's. Look, it's just that a little caution goes a long way out here. These disputes can lead to violence. These objects can still cause people to be killed."

"But by withholding the sacred objects, you're passively participating in a cultural genocide."

Brett remained unflappable. "I know that is how some people view what we're about. We are actively preparing to change our mandate so that repatriation can occur.

"Look, Mark, it's a fraught enterprise, this repatriation business, with unpredictable consequences. We, the whites who've lived in the Centre for years, are still cleansing our eyes of a very recent colonial past. For any dealings out here, and *especially* in matters concerning the Aboriginal sacred life, you must enter into them very carefully, with a practiced intuition. Frankly, it's not a task suited to amateurs. Call me old fashioned, but it's just not the way things are done around here."

At midday, there was still no word from David.

Henk Guth's gallery and museum was set behind a spiked iron fence and a crenelated stucco facade, nostalgic of the European north. The interior decor followed in theme with deeply colored carpeting, dark stained wood paneling dimly lit by tinted glass sconces. Around the perimeter were display cases where the Dutchman housed his personal collection of Aboriginal paraphernalia.

The cases were filled with objects mundane – bowls and boomerangs – to mysterious: emu feather slippers and kneepads worn by a Kadaitcha assassin "to obscure his identity." There was pulverized red ochre molded into a brick and boldly stamped with a spiral, a cockatoo feather headpiece, a collection of "sorcerer's secret wooden pointers" and a chunk of asbestos that "was ground into a fluffy material and adhered with blood to body."

And there were tjurunga. Tjurunga made of wood or stone, laid out as specimens. Some were wrapped round in cords of hairstring. Some were covered tenderly with downy feathers, looking like fledglings fallen out of a nest. One was a slender wooden oval whose ochre patina shone from the polish of handling, and inscribed with tiny circles that floated its length like bubbles in a champagne flute. Next to it was a monster stone, irregular and appearing to be unfinished, yet with a perfect concentric circle gouged deeply into its surface, its bands radiating out to raw edges. Another, a stone platter, bore a diagram that looked like fish eggs clinging to sea grass waving in a gentle current. Complex patterns, road maps into a bizarre intellectual construction.

The boldness of Guth's display should have been a scandal. I had read Lévi-Strauss's *The Savage Mind* on the importance of keeping sacred objects in their rightful place: "for if they were taken out of their place, even in thought, the entire order of the universe would be destroyed." But here was Guth, this bright little man with a rolling Dutch accent, walking among his visitors chirping away about the importance of putting these tjurunga on public view.

"This is the only place in Australia where you can see these stones displayed. No other culture hides their art away. Look at these, they're brilliant." He was right, too; neither the lithographs in turn-of-the-century books nor Reverend Albrecht's rubbings could do justice to the stones' entrancing ornament. "And we take good care of them. These we cover with kangaroo fat," he said, whiffing a hand in front of his nose. "Dat's awful stuff."

He continued talking as we walked. "We have this magnificent culture. We should show people how fine was their work, how rich was their life. You go to Amsterdam and look in the museums. Everything is on display. It's fantastic. And here you get nothing."

I had questions for Guth. "That's secret business," he said. "I'm not allowed to talk about it. You ask too many questions, they come and shoot you. Now look here." He gestured to the case of tjurunga. "That's death. If an Aborigine sees those, that's death."

Did he realize he was contributing to a culture's collapse? He waved his hand at me dismissively. "I bought those tjurungas thirty-five years ago sitting next door in the beer garden. They'd bring these to me and sell them for a flagon of grog."

Later that day I had lunch with an old man named Jeremy Prescott Tjupurula. Prescott was a durable transplant to the Centre – thirty-odd years where four is considered a pretty decent run. He had been a participant-observer in the most important decades of Aboriginal cultural reassertion. He relished his days and nights spent out bush with the old men, had witnessed dozens of restricted ceremonies, was exposed to heaps of sacred material, and was universally respected for the confidences he kept. He had arrived when there was little regard for tribal Law, when the locals dealt with the "Aboriginal problem" themselves, governed by a not too rigid adherence to their own law. He became Alice Springs's most prominent solicitor, helping adherents to traditional law navigate Crown law, and ushering the Aboriginal concept of "sacred sites" into Northern Territory statutes. For all that, on the Queen's birthday when these things are done, he had been awarded the Order of Australia Medal.

Prescott was not impressed with my sanctimonious talk about the inviolability of tjurunga, nor my fretting for the Dreamtime, saying only, "It's a dilemma, that." He described the process of young men's assimilation, not into the ranks of Dreamtime aspirants, but into football. "For the young man, there is the field of engagement, the challenge of a rival team, the potential to rise up by your prowess to be captain – the whole range of stages mocking the path to become a tribal Elder. When given a choice between that and going into the bush for thirty days, cut in various places with a stone knife or an old razor, taught a bunch of mumbo-jumbo, the preferred choice is pretty clear."

That night Karla came home. She dropped her little pack by the door, unlaced a pair of fashionable ankle boots, straightened herself and opened her arms to me. I had just begun to fall into her embrace and respond when she released me and stood back. "I feel maybe you have changed," she said as she stepped around me toward the kitchen. "I think now you are not so fat." She stopped and looked at me. "Tomorrow," she promised, "I will take you on a small excursion to a special place."

An hour's drive west and high up the flank of the MacDonnells, Pine Gap is a pristine nature reserve associated with a long-gone Aboriginal clan. Churning dust seeped through every cranny of Karla's "bush buggy" and hung suspended in the air around us. The road ended at a cul-de-sac. Here, on a picnic table, a proper linen-and-teacakes party was underway for three bonneted ladies from Alice, one pouring from a thermos bottle into china cups.

Karla led me to the reserve's natural gateway, two stout trees, and asked into the space ahead in the traditional manner, for permission to enter. "And now I will take you where I have taken only one other person," she offered in her rich Austrian accent. "Vee vill valk bush."

I followed her into a long glen, over an untrodden path of sand that wound through tall grasses. Natural stone walls rose like waves made fast above us. They swept up, and from their jagged eaves rocks had fallen into scrambled heaps. The waves swelled and crested in succession, rolling down the range in imperceptible geologic time, and this seemed a hallowed place. A breath of air swirled around us and passed down the valley, jostling the grass stalks so they rattled.

After a time, Karla abruptly veered left into the grass and called over her shoulder, "And now you will see the serpent." She disappeared into the brush.

I found her in a shallow cave, bending forward from the low ceiling, stepping out of her panties, her trousers already folded and laid onto a blanket. Bare below her shirttail her flesh was pale, her body slight. A white serpent was painted, its body animate, writhing all along the ceiling. I angled into the cave, smacking my skull against a knob. She reached up, felt for blood then brought me down with her and held me. She urged me with her hands, and had my face between her legs, my hands beneath her shirt on tiny breasts. She tore my hair and made no sound, but afterward caressed me with a kind of joy or thankfulness. We brushed off sand, then settled to watch the last glitter of golden light sifting through the trees, the hour when rocks will flame. Karla gave me wine, and we shared the nuts and the strawberries she had brought along.

When only atmospheric light remained, we climbed to the top of a ridge and settled on the sun-warmed stone. The desert stretched away limitless and flat. Night was pushing away day's remnants of blue while pulling overhead a smattering of stars. Heaven was turning on its spindle, rendering the past, present and future into arbitrary points, all simultaneous and pure potential. Karla and I were courting the inevitable. I turned to her, put my hands on her shoulders to lay her down.

"No, Mark," she said. And then she laughed. "Your face. Look at you, Mark. You take everything so, so seriously."

And she said, "It is okay. Come on then." So I laid her down and was inside. She cried out, startled, and I was consumed as I came.

On the path again, Karla walked beside me, her hand gliding for spirit lines, grass heads brushing her palms. The shapes around us, even in the gloom, were distinct, everything bathed in silver from the near-full moon. I hummed the solemn old hymn "Holy, holy, holy."

Home again, we made supper and fell easily into conversation. While the soup heated she pulled out her project scrapbook, a collection of diagrams shared by cultures worldwide: the net of cartography, the meridians of man and plant. And we talked about the limitations of perception. I told her about my problem with Aboriginal myth stories, that they seemed pointless and often cruel.

"These are not for you," she said. "Those are how this earth speaks to *their* soul. You cannot know as they know. But you receive your own messages from land. You did tell me that on the night we met. You stopped listening. Now the doorway to your heart is opening. I can teach you to listen deeply, to have that clear vision." What I needed was more time than I had to give, more reflection, more walking.

We dipped bread chunks and spooned soup, and there was quiet. Karla set down her spoon. "So stay," she said. She took my unfinished bowl, stacked it on hers, and placed them in the sink. She said, "You should stay."

Day four had passed and yet no word from David.

Day five. They paraded down Todd Mall, a dozen camels strung together nose peg to saddlehorn, laden with drivers' swags and sacks of mail. They were led by bearded men wearing turbans and kaftans, ending their week-long trek from Odnadatta's old railhead. The "Last Mail," a centenary commemoration of the final camel caravan, passed by Karla, myself and the others – Japanese backpackers, Yank military families, school girls whose blue uniform blouses would not stay tucked, buxom butch citizens, and men with broken noses accompanied by toughened young sons. Trailing behind, at the very end of the procession, a children's parade. They carried banners, one stretching across the road proclaimed "Jesus Died For You" and, too heavy for the little child who carried it, a tall cross lettered "Forgiven."

Prayer time at a mosque near Karla's house. I settled into the women's section thinking the back wall would be appropriate for a visiting non-believer. Pulled forward to the men's section, I touched my forehead to the carpet.

Angela took a message for me from David, just back in Alice. He met with some men in Papunya today and has a promising report. Email to follow.

Attended synagogue. Lesson from Exodus. Moses was told by God that he would receive tablets made of stone, written upon by *His Finger*.

Moses climbs the mountain, stays forty days and forty nights while God's engraving of the Law progresses. But below, the Israelites are restive, tired of waiting. They make the Golden Calf. Finally, Moses comes down carrying the tablets. Aghast, angry with his people, he smashes the tablets at their feet.

This night I had a dream. London's Westminster Cathedral, my view is from behind the altar. A procession comes down the central aisle. The pews are full, and people turn to watch the Queen, her robe trailing, dignitaries following. There's a man beside her, his tall frame heaped with shaggy skins. He is carrying a long tubular object, longer than the Royal Scepter. There is a shift in point of view. A close-up. This black man, draped in fur, turns to face the assembly, the vast interior silent, the multitude expectant. He lifts the tube – I can see it better now – moving it slowly to his mouth. He inhales grandly, then blowing through it, he lets out not a musical note but a bellow, like an animal mortally wounded. The cry tumbles down the aisles, strikes the vaulted ceiling like it can crumble stone, and the echo is undying.

Another fully sunny day. Karla, lathered, lay on a chaise. I sat against the tree and sipped beer, reading something or other and peering over the pages at Karla, thinking about her asking me to stay. I couldn't stay out forever, could I? Would she? Among the regrets I carried, my severest rupture, was my divorce. I didn't love Karla as I'd once loved, certainly not in a romantic way, but I was drawn to her more in the manner of a quest, and daring, and growth.

I had family in Texas – scarcely seen, and not as much, perhaps, as they deserve – but no one else at home to tell my story to. I visualized the creekside in Poblado where uncles, aunts, and cousins would assemble, this year as always, in July. If I told them, "The stone is home," would they understand me?

Email from David: "We leave early tomorrow for Papunya. Headman there wants to look at the actual stone. Guardedly optimistic."

Big hug from Karla, "I will wait for you."

19

I STOOD on the curb in the cool pre-dawn, waiting for David to arrive. A folded *Alice Springs News* lay at my feet, easy to read by the light of the moon, now finally full. I looked up, squinting at the brilliance. Headlights swept around the corner, and David's Land Cruiser rushed up the street. He called out his window, "Coming?"

My time in Australia was nearly spent. His man in Papunya was my stone's only remaining hope but one; I could still take a walk and bury the stone in the sand. Theodore Strehlow had written that some old-time Aboriginal men, having no one qualified to receive their sacred objects, had done just that.

We headed north on the Stuart Highway, a road map opened on my lap. As I felt around in my satchel for a penlight, the town's last street lamp passed behind us. David turned left, off the Stuart and onto the Tanami. Now we were driving west, directly toward the moon. It was blinding. Our headlight beams picked at the fence posts ticking past on both sides, and beyond the fence, a blank.

"David, what do we have here with these dots?"

Taking a glance at my map, he replied, "Those would be bores." And rapping a knuckle against his window, "Station country, Aboriginal cattle stations, and communities."

Most of the dots were numbered but some of them had names: Canteen Bore, Spinifex Bore, Eclipse Bore, Expectation Bore. "How about this," I said. "Queen's Visit Bore."

"From the sixties, I reckon, when she was here."

"Came to Adelaide, too. I still have my milk-bottle top. Gold foil. Says 'Queen's Visit.' "

"Bores were put in by the whites maybe a hundred years ago. Give the cattle a drink year round."

The rumm of our tires on the pavement filled the gaps between our talk. Then David asked, "You a Marilyn fan?"

"Marilyn Monroe?"

"Know her film *Bus Stop*?"

"I've seen it."

"So, she's a performer in this saloon out west. Remember the road map she was waving around in her dressing room? It was a map of her 'direction,' the course of her life. She'd drawn three red circles on it." David looked to see if I was following him. "So the camera zooms in far right. First circle is River Gulch, Arkansas. 'That's where I was born,' she says. Thick red line starts there and goes west 'straight as an arrow' to the next circle over Lubbock, Texas, the bus stop. Red line continues. 'Look where I'm going,' she says to her friend. Says it with joy, confident how right her plan is. To the final red circle over Hollywood and Vine cause 'that's where you get discovered, you get optioned.' That's her 'direction.' Because, she said, 'If you don't have direction, you'll just go in circles.' Remember that?"

"No."

"The plan was to go one way, River Gulch to Hollywood and Vine. Then stop. No more going in circles."

"So?"

"Yeah, I'm just pointing out the difference here. Going in circles. That was *their* direction. The circuits, their annual walkabouts. Retrace the creator beings' paths. Do the same next year and the next. Like in cyclic time. Past and future eternally now." David gestured up the road. "The men you'll meet later today, they were drawn out of the desert. Followed in a chain of bores. In Papunya, their journeying stopped."

The moon outpaced us, slipping below the horizon just as the first blast of sunlight launched our car's shadow ahead of us. David slowed down at a turn-off.

The hum in our car became a racket as we chattered down a washboard track, weaving a little over the corrugations. David lifted one finger to salute an oncoming car. We overtook a lorry on whose open bed stood half a dozen women powdered in white, swaying in unison against the rails like milk bottles in a crate. "Sorry business. A lot of deaths from alcohol. Car accidents, fighting." We gave up talking. Kangaroo bodies lay on the roadside, limbs wrenched akimbo, explanation enough for the "roo bars" across the front of David's car. Then there was nothing for the longest time.

We pulled to a stop. I stepped away from the car to pee, watching the countryside materialize as my senses cleared. I was looking into a new world. Ranchland, no longer fenced and featureless, was now a many-hued landscape of wildflowers carpeting the sandy loam. I counted seven varieties in blue, yellow, a dark pink, and apricot. The air was scented with lavender and salt. And every few steps brought us to another garden of flowers.

The void left by the racket of driving was slowly filled with choruses of bird song. A flock of lime-green parrots streaked close over our heads. "It's the desert at its finest," David whispered, as though a tone of exuberance would embarrass this blush of life. After the heaviest rains they'd had in thirty years, all life was suddenly in a hurry.

He named the acacia and mulga trees and their features, distinguishing varieties in the same family, and the bushes and ground covers. He identified birds and ants known as markers for desirable bush tucker. We watched as Willie Wagtails darted in and out of a majestic fig tree whose branches dropped fruit to desiccate on a rock outcrop, no people here to compete for edibles with the birds and the insects that joined in this swelling of life.

Stepping forward, David said, "I know this place. Mark, fancy a stroll?"

The land nearby was drawn up into jagged rocky hills that grew steadily in stature as we approached. A cleft opened, and we walked in. Stone walls, the color of bloody meat, jutted abruptly out of the sand. In this shadowed and intimate space, the water-polished walls radiated nighttime's chill. I stepped through a fringe of grass to touch the stone, smooth as cordovan leather. As my hand swept along a shelf of rock, I found a little design pecked into the surface, worn down but clearly it was a nest of concentric circles. This was when I realized I had left my tjurunga stone sitting in the unlocked car.

"David," I called ahead to him.

"Yeah," he replied without turning, "there's some more up here." The rock where he stood was flat and wide as a table. It was strewn with these diagrams. "This is an old campsite."

"David, I'm afraid someone will take my tjurunga."

"Have a look behind those grasses over there."

I followed his pointing finger to the opposite wall and pushed the grass stalks aside with my shoe. On the ground was a stone worn flat and smooth, and on top of it another, shaped like a tapered rolling pin. "You won't often find those out here," David said as he came beside me. "Most were pinched for curios, which pissed the Aboriginal women. They'd leave their grinders at each campsite."

"David, we should go back now."

He pulled a wooden object, two feet long, out of the thicket. It was oval-shaped and carved into a shallow trough, but fractured and obviously had been discarded long ago.

"The tjurunga," I said, pointing toward the canyon's outlet.

"A coolamon," David said in reply.

Stepping to the center of the sand bed, David dropped to his knees. He lifted up the coolamon then cuffed at the ground. Drawing the sand toward him, he widened the hole even as sand slid back into his excavation. He kept at it, deepening the pit, the sand darkening and coming up in cohesive scoops.

"David, I'm not ready for this. This won't do," I said.

With a line of sweat along his brow, he sat back on his heels and tossed the tool aside. He looked at what he had done and smiled. A little pool of water collected at the bottom. He stood and with a gesture out of chivalry, he said, "G'won, Mark. Have a drink on me." I pushed my nose into the damp hole, swished and spat. "Okay, David, you're a dinkum bushman." I picked out the grains I had taken in.

But this place *will* do, I thought, as David started up the car. If it doesn't go well in Papunya, I'll bring the stone back here and bury it up this canyon by the other relics. As we gained speed, our hill was soon lost, indistinguishable from the others, perfectly anonymous.

According to the map, we were near Papunya: past the Thelma Bore on the right and, on the left, the turn-off to Haasts Bluff. Papunya was a black dot with a little circle around it.

"The name translates as *this meeting place is shared*," he said, "which is appropriate because there's a lot of different tribes there now. It was built in the sixties over a honey ant Dreaming site, an old ceremonial center. It's now basically a refugee camp."

The settlement had been graded out of the desert, he explained, to contain Aboriginals who had overwhelmed the barrier line of missionary food depots in a time of mass dislocation. Papunya was a desperate initiative to protect these people from total loss. The resources for the internees had been spartan: rations and bore water, and these days, welfare – "sit down money." It would be amazing, I thought, if any traditions had survived.

David downshifted. On both sides of the road lay a galaxy of sequins, a Milky Way of broken glass, glittering brilliantly in green and yellow and red.

"Grog," he said. "The lands are dry. Last swig and out the window it goes."

"Now, David, about these Elders. They know what we're about?"

"Yeah, I called ahead yesterday. We're expected. We're welcome to come in. After that, we'll see."

"You've done this before?"

"Just once."

"And how'd that go?"

"It didn't. I showed it to the men but they didn't want it. Said it came from another people up northwest. I took it to Kintore but no one there recognized it either. It's in the shop until someone claims it."

"The shop?"

"Yeah, Land Council bought a jeweler's shop. Nice big safe. It's where we keep the orphans."

We passed through a field of little huts, just corrugated iron sheets bent over and left open-ended. "Wurlies," David said. "The council provides a cement house. But the families are always moving out. The wind'll blow, a door slams, they think it's a spirit and off they go."

Then we were in Papunya. No gate, no signpost of welcome or prohibition, just blocks of tin-roofed buildings. Grim, a scar on the surface of the desert: snagged plastic bags, spindly trees casting leafless shade, and in front of the Council office building, the grass brittle as shards. We stood beside the Land Cruiser and beat the dust from our laps.

Under the verandah, on the cement slab, two Aboriginal women sat in fiberglass bucket seats, looking past us, chattering. We were the only whites. No one seemed to care when David brought a stranger in through the open double-doors.

At the front desk, David greeted the men he knew with a handshake, reminding each when they had last met and rechecking their skin-clan names, "Tjupurrula, right? No? Tjangala. Right."

Chris Bowman strolled up wearing his extra-broad brimmed felt hat. "You're the Yank?" he said to me. "How's it going? G'day, David." Handshakes all around. Chris was the schoolteacher and the only white in permanent residence. His tenacity was remarkable, having lived in Papunya for twenty years. Geoffrey Bardon, his predecessor, had held his position for only one. Both men's experiences in Papunya were veined with personal bitterness and resentment towards the Territory government. "Dismissive and detestable," is how Bardon had put it. And Chris, "Not even a bloody shelter for the painters."

David asked Chris to help us collect the Elders who would preside over the presentation of my stone. He walked off for his vehicle to round up three of them. David and I drove to the store to collect some food, an offering, and from there we would pick up the other two.

The store, running strictly on cashed welfare checks, sold red meat packages, shrink-wrapped vegetables, sugary juices and frozen pizza. It was a general store so there were also some basic auto parts, shoes – which seemed as little desired in Papunya as the children's yellow floatation wings – a dusty guitar, and a framed portrait of Jesus Christ cradling his Sacred Heart. David filled a box with cold drinks, and I contributed two packages of Arnott's Family Assorted Crème Filled Biscuits. For myself, I picked out a roll of film whose expiration date had passed more recently than others on the rack.

At the checkout I asked Karen, the lady at the register, about the local diet.

"I buy the food they want – tea, kangaroo tails, and sugar. Lots of sugar. Some have switched to Saccharin. The sugar's killing them."

"Kangaroo *tails?*" I asked.

"Yeah, the women love them."

"Where do they come from, these tails?"

"Oh, wherever you get rain you'll get kangaroos by the zillions. These were shot at the King River Station. Sent to Perth for processing. That's 3000 kilometers. And back here on the supply truck, that's another 2000. So the tails have traveled a bit. The ladies throw them on the fire and carry them around for hours. Chew, chew, chew."

"Occasionally," David added, "the men'll go out and shoot a roo. Once I saw four men carrying four back in. Cooked em on the edge of the settlement and polished them off. A kangaroo each! Their women could see the men were having a feed, but they won't go over to ask for some. It's not done."

David backed his car carefully out between the clumps of squatting women and milling children, then turned toward the residences. We pulled up at a house where an old gentleman sat beside a smoldering fire, and alongside it there was a bundle of six-foot-long sticks. He had one gripped in his teeth as he pulled back on the two ends, apparently to straighten it. Not satisfied, he rotated the shaft's kink over the coals for a minute longer then brought it back to his mouth.

"G'day, Old Albert. That's lookin good."

He raised his eyes to David without loosening his bite.

"You're a champion, aren't you Albert?" And to me, "Bush Olympics. Old Albert's a champion. Aren't you, Albert, a champion spear thrower?"

The gentleman set aside his work and pulled on a greasy denim shirt, the sleeves already rolled up to the elbow. He topped off with his black western hat, banded with silver buttons. This was Old Albert

Tjakamarra, the senior man at Papunya. My rush to Australia, my fear that the last of the traditional men were about to die off, I guess, had been overwrought. Old Albert looked rather well.

"We'll find Mick and meet the others at the museum?" David proposed.

When Albert rose to join us, the eyes that met mine showed nothing more than forbearance. He was tolerating my presence and that was all, but he was clearly on board.

We found Mick outside his cinderblock house sitting in the dirt, a look of contentment on his face. His legs were sprawled before him, one over each of his dogs, and behind him in a huddle women were playing cards. No one, not even the dogs, reacted as he left.

We gathered a little speed and left the settlement behind, our tires lifting a plume of the desert's fine sand.

I did not want us to meet at some museum as David had suggested but instead out in the wild at some enchanted place. Mount Larrie, only ten kilometers further along the track, would do just fine. I had read about Mount Larrie in a book written by the American Elizabeth Dean: "The hills were covered with trees like cloves in a Virginia-baked ham."

In the 1950s she had ventured west of Papunya, into the ranges over which Mt. Larrie presides. As a modern dancer and choreographer, she was interested in how dance had been incorporated into ritual. This is what I had in mind for my reception, her words:

> The men were chanting now. This grew louder and louder, finally to break into a triumphal burst of utter joy, just as the first faint light of dawn touched the surrounding hills. Simultaneously, running figures, in profuse decorations of feathers, ochre and the delicacy of white and blood-red feather down, came plummeting out of the bush from different angles of the compass, each holding before him a treasured tjurunga gorgeously decked in alternating bars of red and white down, with emu feather tufts at the top. It was pure theater.

Dean had choreographed her interpretation of native "theater" and presented it in Sydney as *Corroboree*. In attendance was Queen Elizabeth. The performance, it was said, inspired Her Majesty to travel to Alice Springs, during her second Australian visit. The artistic goal Ms. Dean set for herself was to see and "feel" Aboriginal dance culture "before it is all gone, for as the young aboriginal men come more and more into our 'white fellow' ways…."

Before I could voice my preference, the museum came into view.

"That used to be the museum," David said as we sped past. Four corrugated iron sheds around a hidden inner yard, all of it surrounded by a rusty chain-link fence.

"*That* was a museum?"

"It wasn't that kind of museum," David replied. "It was a keeping place for the tjurunga, for ritually correct men. Isn't that right, Old Albert? A men's-business place?"

David added, "The sacred objects were moved."

A little way out of town, we pulled up behind Chris's car. There was a clearing in the scrub around a patch of charred sand, and nothing else except two tipped-over steel barrels. It was a dump. As we came closer, I saw that one end of each barrel was welded to the other, making one long, sealed vessel. A torched-off segment of the body had been hinged and set back on as a lid, then secured with a padlock.

David and I carried the cookies and drinks out of his car and set them down. Chris named the men for me as they settled onto the ground: Old Albert, Gill Tjungurrayi, Mervyn Tjangala and Mick Tjampitjinpa. Johnny Tjupurulla pulled up a chrome car wheel whose rubber had been burnt to the rim and sat on it, completing our circle. The tjurunga stone was inside the satchel tucked underneath my crossed legs.

David began the meeting. "Mark here is from America wanting to talk about a tjurunga. I've got that photo. You've seen this one already, the last time I came."

"You bin showin that one," Old Albert said. Acknowledgment echoed in the round: "yuwaa, yuwaa."

"Mark didn't want to put it in a museum in Adelaide or Melbourne. He wanted to bring it back to a smaller museum, a proper one."

He brought the Xerox out and asked. "Is that alright that we look at the photo?"

Albert said, "You can show em again," and David passed the paper to his left. A flood of Luritja words, entirely lost on me, accompanied it on its way around the circle.

When the Xerox reached Mick, he ground his index finger into the central spiral and then to another, tap-tapping at them as he looked to Albert. He said, "Papunya, Papunya. Honey ant Dreaming. This one here." He passed the sheet over to Johnny who gave it mute scrutiny and handed it on. Chris whispered, "Johnny's the youngest. He's being brought into the tradition. That's why he's here." The men seemed to have forgotten that David, Chris and I existed.

When the photo came back around to Albert, he lay it on his lap and bent forward extending his hand to the ground. He picked a few little sticks out of the sand and flattened the surface as smooth as slate. The men sat silently as they watched. Deliberately yet fluidly, his finger made out a perfect circle, about twelve inches across. Inside, he drew a spiral coiling inward. With a deft twist of his fingertip he made a small rounded head. The motion of his hand was mirrored by its black shadow, which seemed to glide under the sand, drawing upwards.

~rt paused to look to the men around him and read their silence. With a casual swipe, he obliterated his map. "Honey ant Dreaming," said Albert in English, sweeping his hand through the air and across the land around us. "He not from different country."

"No, this land here," Gill pronounced.

And Albert again, "This one here, Papunya."

Mick contributed, "Honey ant Dreaming."

Albert asked, "Alright?" The men nodded assent and chuckles of relief rippled around the circle.

Albert addressed David, "That's what we're talking about, you know? Askin em this tjurunga. Papunya, alright? We can make arrangements with that one. Somebody got to bring up that one. Anytime." There it was: mythology, land, and custodianship. They had done it. I had done it. This stone would not be leaving. It was home, or rather, it was in my satchel.

The question came from Johnny, "You got it here?"

"Yeah," I said. Once it left my hands, I would have no further rights to it. This would be an irrevocable transfer of custody.

Albert said, "Where you got em?"

Reaching into my satchel, I pulled it out and handed it over to Albert. With both hands, he lifted the stone up and examined it. The engravings looked shallow, not as clearly defined as I remembered. Adjusting the stone with a clockwise twist and a slight tilt upward, Albert set it at an angle to the sun's raking light. The banding of the spirals sank into its surface like the furrows of a just-plowed field. The stone's faint pink color deepened into rust red, as though flushing with warmth. Around me there was rapid and urgent discussion. A fly buzzed past my head. And then Albert nodded gently up and down.

He lowered the stone, enclosing it in his hands, and the tips of his fingers glided over its surface. He gently traced the spiral, following the journey inward to its center. From that spiral's node, his fingers cut to the neighboring figure and then down again to find its center.

"He's uncovering the Dreaming," David said. I looked to Chris to explain. "Like a doused fire, a Dreaming story can be extinguished when its tjurunga is gone."

Albert's fingers retraced the mythic honey ant's journey across the land until each site had been touched and vitalized, and his memory of the tjurunga's Dreamtime story was drawn into the present.

"What a man can keep in his heart and memory is important," Chris whispered. "But it's only when you get men together that the story is told, reinforced and transmitted."

Albert was mumbling to himself, but as his hand returned to the center of the stone and the large spiral, throaty utterances resolved into distinct phrases. Gill and Mick's voices joined him for a few lines, and then all the voices dropped away.

Referring to the honey ant, or possibly to the stone, Albert said quietly, almost to himself, "Him travellin a long way."

David, turning to me, said, "You might like to tell the story about how you came to be involved." And to the circle at large, "Would it be alright if Mark told a bit of a story about how he got the tjurunga?" Nods of assent came from each man.

I began, "Back in 1960, my family moved to Adelaide from America." I told of Dad's buying the stone in Hermannsburg, and the tale of its theft from Uluru. Then I paused.

The men broke into commentary, replaying my words in Luritja and reconstructing the events so that they all understood what had been said, so that everyone heard the story correctly. A bird was chirping from a branch near by. "Keep goin," came the command.

"So, he took it home," and reaching the end of my account, "I brought the stone back here." Hearing my story, it must have sounded so simple and inevitable to these men: Of course, this is what one does. Why would you keep something that doesn't belong to you? I wrapped it all up quickly. "So I am very pleased to do what my father wanted and to bring it back where it belongs." I let it rest at that.

Albert said, "He did the right thing." He fixed me with his eyes. "That's a long way to come. Thank you for bringin it." Sweat-stained hats nodded in assent around the circle.

Attention turned then to a practical problem. The lid hinged to the steel drum was secured by a padlock. But since the men were last out here the key had been lost. The sacred objects inside could not be retrieved if needed for a ceremony and neither could another be placed inside. The man in town who owned a bolt-cutter had left with the device, and the hacksaw blade was broken. David rummaged in the back of his Land Cruiser while everyone else stood around helpless. He produced a file, a jack, a shovel, and a didgeridoo.

Chris, unperturbed, drove back to town to look once more for the bolt cutter. We dragged over the box of drinks and cookies and sat down again.

Gill asked David about the Strehlow Research Centre in Alice Springs, "Strehlow museum. How much money they make?"

"They don't sell objects or anything like that. They have some tjurunga there that came from Ted Strehlow after he died. He passed them on to his son and his boy put them there for safe-keeping." One of the men recalled seeing Strehlow on camelback in '42.

Another of the men asked David, "Aboriginal people getting them from the Strehlow Centre?" David was slow to reply, and the man protested. "Those things there, they belong to the Aboriginal ones."

"Yeah," said David, "that's right."

Chris returned from the Council office with the bolt-cutter, and the quickly severed body of the lock was hurled into the brush. Just at that moment, a snake was spotted in the tall grass near the barrels. The alarm went up, "Snake cheeky bugger!" Mick leaped up to chase it away, and I plunged ahead with my camera angled down. The snake eluded both of us and, when we returned, the circle of men had broken up. The steel lid on the barrel banged down. With the new lock snapped closed, Albert handed both keys to Chris. "You keep these. I'll be losing em again."

The party dispersed and cars rolled back into town to drop the men at their homes. David, Chris and I met up at Chris's house.

I asked, "Chris, these men wouldn't accept a stone they didn't have rights over, would they?"

"It's not unheard of. They'd just lock them away not knowing what to do with em. They'd be in a kind of moral bind: 'we understand that we should take care of them because we are living here on this land, but we can't use them because we don't know the songs, and they're not ours."

"What will happen now, to this stone, the one I brought?"

"I think it will be largely limited to curiosity value. The men will look at it from time to time and enjoy speculating about its history and so forth, but I doubt it'll ever be used again for religious purposes. They might sell it if they wanted to. They have the right. You blokes staying for dinner?"

My flight was leaving Alice Springs in six hours.

In David's car, on the way back to town, I stared out the windscreen, the tjurunga stone no longer at my feet. We shared a good meander, and I missed the little bugger already. Karla's sofa-bed had come as close to home as I had felt in quite a while but there had been no more talk of my staying. I was free now, and had only myself to think of.

Had Old Albert been doing the "good whitefella" thing by taking charge of a stone that was not his? I couldn't say; the stone's return was somewhat unresolved. But if Old Albert sincerely wanted that stone, that was good enough for me, and more than my father could have hoped. I was satisfied that the tjurunga had been received by five Elders, all of them upright and well-respected men. They had the knowledge, and they used it. For myself, I hoped that there would be a young man in the Centre to hold that thing in his hands, to learn about the devotion of his fathers.

In Central Australia, the humblest fragment of the earth, a tjurunga stone, revealed itself as sacred, and all nature and the cosmos in its entirety likewise revealed itself to Aboriginals as sacred. From my point of view, Old Albert's sacred stone was just a fragment of the Dreamtime's ruin. For Old Albert, the spirit in the stone was not contingent. Even if a scouring by the Finke River were to render this tjurunga indistinguishable from all other stones, the spirit in the object, and the land I am told, remains; out in this desert, circulating in vast currents below the surface, a mystic essence abides.

While sitting with Michael on his "grandfather's" ledge at Kata Tjuta, the precipice overlooking the valley of orange stupas, I was made vividly aware that we live in eternity. And there had been Karla, walking among the boulders, who asked me, "Do you feel it?" She said, "It's stronger here." On the sand path out of the reserve at Pine Gap, I had sensed ancient footsteps that descended alongside us. Here, in the Centre, my spirit yearned to project itself onto this landscape, into a living unknown. I felt a beckoning.

D AVID KEPT his land cruiser idling in Karla's driveway, poised to hustle me to the Alice aerodrome. Karla was late for a client rendezvous, so there was hardly a minute to look full into the other's eyes. I felt like I was running away, and I said as much.

She took hold of my shirt button, the one nearest my throat, and gently rubbed it between her fingers saying, "If we started up a baby," then she yanked on the button and pulled me to her face, "you will hear from me." She kissed me then, hard on the mouth. She didn't release me or turn away this time. I was more than a little surprised. David *beep beeped* his horn. "It is okay," she said. "You should go."

I carried my bag down the driveway to the car. David pushed my door open, and I sat. I had one foot inside and the other still on the red earth when Karla stepped out and called, "Did you get what you wanted, the thing you came for?"

David looked at me, looked at his watch. My eyes were fixed on Karla. Hers were reading mine. David reached for the ignition and switched off the motor. He sat back and massaged his eyes.

AFTERWORD

I was surprised when John invited me to write this Afterword for Sacred Errand. After all, I was the Director of the Strehlow Research Centre in Alice Springs who, as figured in his book, had strongly advised against repatriation of the tjurunga at the Rock Art Congress held in Alice Springs. The attitude that the book's fictional narrator, Mark, carried was actually John's: that you can just give cultural objects back. That was the prevailing perception. But there is always more to deal with for both the party in possession and the recipient. John's epic adventure in Australia became a journey into his soul.

Through John, his "father's tjurunga" made its way to Papunya and into the hands of traditional Aboriginal custodians who securely stowed it away. In the book's final pages Mark meditates on his journey, writing that he had been made aware at Kata Tjuta that "we live in eternity" and at Pine Gap that he had "sensed ancient footsteps that descended alongside us." These are the self-revelatory, even epiphanic, gifts that were delivered to Mark in the form of the tjurunga.

Tjurunga carry the spirit of a creation- or totemic ancestor that once travelled the land. Aboriginal people in Central Australia have that same spirit abiding in them. They are in that sense one and the same. The human body, just as the stone or wood from which a tjurunga is created, is more or less a vessel through which the spirit flows in a cycle of reincarnation. The tjurunga is as alive as a person is alive.

In the closing moments of Mark's story, why then weren't Old Albert and those other old Aboriginal men especially moved at the moment of the return of the tjurunga midst the red dust and flies of Papunya? Because they had long ago been on that revelatory pilgrimage which, unbeknownst to him, Mark had also been traversing.

Brett Galt-Smith

The author out bush in Central Australia

ABOUT THE AUTHOR

John Harkey's *Sacred Errand* was first presented as an illustrated lecture series sponsored by the Rhode Island Council For The Humanities. John previously received a National Endowment For The Humanities grant to produce the photographic exhibition *San Antonio, What is at Issue?*, which examined historic and contemporary social issues of that city.

Raised overseas and in Texas, Harkey has lived in Spain and Argentina with his wife Ginger, a returned Peace Corps volunteer to Sierra Leone and a retired ESL and Spanish bilingual teacher. They now reside in Providence, Rhode Island. Their two children Abigail and Jeremy share an interest in indigenous cultures, and each received a Metcalf grant from the Rhode Island Foundation to pursue independent research in Ecuador and Australia.

The author's father, a geophysicist, led his young family to Libya, then to Australia where *Sacred Errand* had its beginnings. Harkey's mother was an artist and professional musician, employed as a church organist wherever the family landed.

Harkey is a graduate of the Rhode Island School of Design (MFA '78) and is a retired, award-winning commercial photographer. His fine art photographs are in the collections of the Dallas Museum of Art, and the Amon Carter Museum of American Art.

Sacred Errand is Harkey's first book.